TROUBLE ON THE BRAZOS

TROUBLE ON THE BRAZOS

Will C. Brown

Chivers Press ● G.K. Hall & Co.
Bath, England   Thorndike, Maine USA

This Large Print edition is published by Chivers Press, England, and by G.K. Hall & Co., USA.

Published in 2000 in the U.K. by arrangement with Golden West Literary Agency.

Published in 2000 in the U.S. by arrangement with Golden West Literary Agency.

U.K. Hardcover ISBN 0-7540-4018-6   (Chivers Large Print)
U.S. Softcover   ISBN 0-7838-8850-3   (Nightingale Series Edition)

A shorter version of this novel appeared in RANCH ROMANCES Magazine.

The text of this Large Print edition is unabridged.
Other aspects of the book may vary from the original edition.

Set in 16 pt. New Times Roman.

Printed in Great Britain on acid-free paper.

British Library Cataloguing in Publication Data available

Library of Congress Cataloging-in-Publication Data

Brown, Will C., 1905–
       Trouble on the Brazos / by Will C. Brown.
       p.   cm.
       ISBN 0-7838-8850-3 (lg. print : sc : alk. paper)
       1. Frontier and pioneer life—Texas—Fiction.
       2. Large type books.   I. Title.
PS3552.R739 T76   2000
813'.54—dc21   99–055722

CHAPTER ONE

Soon after sunup Rotan came into the shack and took the Winchester off the wall pegs, so Trav knew that they were going to call on the nester.

It was a chilly Cap Rock morning in early April and this whole upper part of Texas was showing a touch of brave greenery after bleak months of blue northers and howling winter sandstorms. Trav sat upright on the cot, watched Rotan's heavy movements for a moment, and then threw the blanket aside.

It was a faded Confederate blanket, long ago stolen by a Tonkawa buck, re-stolen later by somebody along the Chisholm Trail, and recently appropriated by Rotan as a part of his money's worth after a night's lodging in the loft of a wagon yard. The blanket now lay on the splintered floor planking like a threadbare remnant of the lives of men unknown and of the troubled sleep it might have covered on nights stretching back through many valleys of darkness. Casting the blanket aside was, for Trav Parker, a signal of decision.

Rotan stiffened.

'Just me,' he said. 'You ain't going.'

Trav examined his wound. The bandage showed no new stain this morning. The place had healed. It felt all right. He pulled on his

1

boots, limped over and got his gunbelt, and picked up his hat. Rotan kept a frown locked on these proceedings.

'The nester came back, did he?' Trav asked.

'You got no business going.'

'Don't tell me what my business is,' Trav snapped.

'For somebody with no blood,' the shaggy Rotan growled, 'you're feelin' your oats right strong.'

'I've got blood to spare,' Trav retorted. 'You let me worry about that. What did this hombre look like?'

'Poison.'

'You see him good?'

'Naw. But he's a Cap Rock nester, so I know he looks like poison.'

Trav chuckled softly. 'He didn't spot you, did he?'

'I was on my belly in the brush and there was a mile stretch of mesquites between us. I couldn't see much. He drove up to his place in a wagon and then went to the house. That's all I saw.'

'Just one man, eh?'

'Just him.'

'What kind of wagon?'

'I dunno. Swayback and wheels wobblin'. Typical homesteader wagon. Why?'

'Covered?'

'Yeah.'

Trav moved impatiently. 'Then how do you

2

know what was under the cover? How do you know there was just this one man?'

'Godamighty, you're cactusy today. What you expect him to have under the wagon sheet—six grown sons?'

'It's possible.' Then Trav said quietly: 'Gus Jenkins. If we guessed right. It's been a long time. We've ridden a lot of miles.'

'Don't count no chickens. But I guess it's Jenkins, all right.'

'Well, let's get at it. The horses saddled?'

'What for?' Rotan demanded. 'This is a foot job. And it's a long crawl through the brush. You oughtn't to try it. I can take Jenkins myself, then you can come on down.'

'No crawling.' Trav paused at the door and smiled onesidedly. 'You sound like a fugitive. I'm sick of crawling. What are we, a couple of damned tarantulas?'

'Could be. We ain't had a shave in two weeks. No, three. We been following the Brazos three weeks. What'd you mean we don't crawl?'

'We visit this jasper head-on. What's wrong with two innocent transients riding up to his house and passing the time of day with an honest man?'

'Nothing a-tall, unless the honest man's holding a gun on you. These nesters don't like nobody, which is why they're up here in the first place.'

'Quit being so jumpy.'

3

When they mounted, Rotan watched the way Trav swung into the saddle. Trav tried to disguise a grimace brought on by the pull of dull pain and pretended that his leg muscle didn't burn with the movement. In another minute, they rode through the greening mesquites and plump cedars, walking their horses. The route lay downgrade to a rocky draw, upgrade again through more brush, and onto the flats toward the nester place.

Trav felt the need to say only one thing on the ride.

'I'll do the talking. No rough business, unless he makes it rough.'

They rode on in silence, in sight now of the gaunt parade of rocks and low cliffs that formed the peculiar upthrusts of the Texas Cap Rock. This eroded cliff line straggled westward from the narrow cut of the upper Brazos River. If Texas had been a tree, with its roots in the Rio Grande, this country would be its high-up branches, where habitation thinned out to the open sky. The vastness of the Llano Estacado here began its mighty sweep northwestward. Comanche country. Rich with grass and buffalo meat, but wearing its Cap Rock ridges like a giant's challenging bootheel line drawn against any settler thinking to cross the Brazos. Here was new land, an eternity of it disappearing into the Panhandle, into New Mexico, and God knew where, and into its mysterious distances Trav Parker had come at

4

last in search of one man.

Now his attention centered alertly upon the nester clearing taking outline ahead. He hoped Jenkins would make no mean show out of this. He loosened his sixgun as he neared the rim of cut brush. Rotan, behind him, had the rifle, and it might have been wiser to carry the Winchester on the first horse. But Trav knew a suspenseful urge to be the one to lead the way to this meeting with Gus Jenkins. And as he gave the nester house his full concentration, he almost missed the small, dark movement behind the dead brush to his right.

So fast that Trav barely had time to drag out his sixgun, a man who was stretched full length behind the brush pile floundered about to face the two riders, swung his rifle and triggered a hasty shot. The too-quick bullet sang sizzling past Trav's head. The hand on the rifle desperately pumped a new round, but Trav's gun leveled on him. It was extreme range for the .45 and he forced himself to fix the aim with patience. The second rifle bullet and his squeezed off sixgun slug blasted out at each other in the same instant. The rifleman lazily relaxed, turned his gun loose, and then lay in the fully inert shape a dead man so quickly takes.

Rotan barked, 'What the hell?'

'Keep a lookout. Damn him, why did he make me do that?'

'Was that nester trying to ambush us?'

'Not us.' Trav pointed. 'He was gunning for the house. He got panicky when we rode up. Now, who would he be? Not Jenkins.'

'He's not anybody, now.'

'Watch it. There's Jenkins coming out of his house.'

Trav rode over and looked at the ambusher. He saw a nondescript face, two holstered guns, and blood soaking the shirt front. 'Somebody didn't like Jenkins. Let's go for the house, now—and keep alive. We don't know which way Jenkins is going to jump.'

They pulled their mounts a little distance apart, riding into the bare yard, spreading Jenkins' attention but careful to make no hostile move. Jenkins stood on the edge of the small porch, his rifle ready, alertly taking them in. Whichever way the man jumped, Trav thought, he and Rotan would have to jump a shade ahead of him.

He smiled disarmingly at the upturned, middle-aged face.

'Sorry to bust in on you with so much noise. A fellow behind the brush over there seemed to be set for a shot at something in this direction.' He pushed his hat back half an inch with a slow, easy motion.

Jenkins cut his eyes quickly toward the brush and back again. He licked his upper lip. The man had more intelligence in his creviced features than Trav had expected to see. A kind of remote dignity showed behind his pale,

6

wind reddened eyes.

But a shock, or an unpleasant realization, showed also. The nester seemed to be adding up the story of the shots. Finally he spoke.

'Did you get him?'

'I did.' Trav nodded soberly. 'He gave me no chance to do anything else.'

The man thought that over, too. He said one word. 'Thanks.'

'Yeah.'

'What did you want here?'

'Why, my friend and I are just riding across the country. Saw your place. We ran short of grub a while back.'

'Do I know you?'

'I guess not. We're strangers up here.'

He saw the rifle lower in Jenkins' hand. 'I guess I owe you a meal. Come on in.'

It was going to be easier than Trav had thought. Jenkins, while not exactly friendly, was at least being civil. Trav felt almost reluctant. But he gave Rotan an imperceptible nod and they made their move.

As Jenkins turned to reach for the door catch, Trav brought his sixgun up and rammed the muzzle hard into his back. In the same instant, Rotan tore the rifle from Jenkins' hand and pulled his revolver from its holster.

'Just go right on in, now,' Trav said. 'Don't make any sudden moves, Jenkins.'

The closing door sealed them in the dim

7

light of a sparsely furnished room. A coffee pot puffed busily on a small iron stove. A side of salt-crusted bacon and a butcher knife lay on the pine counter at the kitchen end of the room. An unmade bunk in the corner showed where Jenkins had slept through a thinly-blanketed night.

Rotan sniffed. 'Coffee! Glory be!'

Jenkins held his watchful gaze on the younger of the intruders while Rotan hovered over the stove.

'What is it you want?'

Trav said, 'Sit down, Jenkins.'

'I'll stand.'

'No, you'll sit. From here on you're doing what I say do.'

Jenkins muttered, 'High-handed.'

'Very. Go on, friend—sit down.'

Jenkins sat stiffly on the edge of his bunk. Trav eased himself into a rope-bottomed chair and gingerly felt of his leg bandage.

Rotan called over, 'You want biscuits and sowbelly?'

Trav watched the ramrod-stiff Jenkins. 'I always like to have a polite invitation before I eat.'

The nester's jaws worked. 'Help yourself.'

'All right, Rotan. Sowbelly, biscuits, gravy and coffee. Fry the grease out of the sowbelly. Maybe he's got molasses, too.'

He made himself relax a little, but he kept feeling the inner nervousness. Here he was, face to face with Gus Jenkins. He took off his hat, holstered his gun, and gave his attention to making a smoke. Studying his fingers, he saw that they showed no tremble. He drew his lungs full of smoke. He tasted it deeply and savored its leafy burn again as he let the smoke flow out.

'The first thing for you to get in your head, Jenkins, is that all we want from you, besides a bait of breakfast, is a little talk. Maybe it would slack your rope if I told you right off, you're not going to get hurt. At least, that's our intent. That'll be up to you.'

Trav waited. Jenkins held his stare.

He mumbled, 'You'd a never made a break-in on me except for that shootin'. It fooled me. Well, what is it you want?'

'That shooting, friend, was no fooling. There was a man laying for you. We'll take you up there after a while and you can see if you know the gent.' Travs voice went harsh. 'Why is it, Jenkins, that somebody decided he wanted you dead?'

He might be rushing this, Trav tried to caution himself. But every nerve bristled with the compelling desire to know. He was conscious that Rotan had stopped his movements and had drawn nearer, watching and listening.

Jenkins moistened his lips again. 'I never saw you before. I don't know why you're doing this.'

9

Trav leaned forward. He spoke slowly. 'A man named Gus Jenkins made a herd drive to Kansas once. You're the Gus Jenkins who made that trail trip, and coming back you rode with a man named Jack Hinton. Somewhere in the Territory, another rider bound for Texas was shot and left for dead and sixty thousand dollars were stolen off of him. I was the man who lost the herd money, Jenkins, and damn near my life. You were the man who was with the Jack Hinton outfit, and you are the first and only one of them I've been able to get trace of. Wait a minute—don't say anything yet. Don't say anything till this sinks deep in your brain. There's just one thing I want, Jenkins. I reckon you ought to know that I want it bad enough to do anything to get it, and that includes putting a bullet through you if I have to.'

Jenkins' eyes looked old and his expression went haggard. A slump of defeat came over the man's whole raggedy frame.

'What I want to know, Jenkins, is this: *where is Jack Hinton?*'

In the long silence, Trav watched the small beads of sweat fever out on Jenkins' lined forehead. The coffee pot hummed pleasantly on the stove. Rotan stayed planted beside Trav's chair.

'If I told you that,' Jenkins mumbled helplessly, 'I'd get killed.'

Trav twisted and shot a glance up to Rotan.

10

The bewhiskered head nodded back to him.

'You've told me one thing, Jenkins,' Trav murmured. 'I think you've just admitted that you know where Jack Hinton is. The rest we'll get out of you, all right.'

Trav gouged words at him. 'You know where he is. You just don't have any choice left, friend. Maybe he's going to kill you if you talk, but I'm damn sure going to kill you if you don't talk. You just sit there and be making up your mind while I have a slug of your coffee.'

'You've got it a little wrong, stranger.' Jenkins jerked his chin to indicate the brush beyond the clearing. 'That likely was a caller from the man you want, out there. The way I put that together is, he's heard you're on my trail. If he has, I'll tell you straight, you haven't got a chance. You and me both are goners.'

Trav knew, then, with the first hair crinkle of alarm and the small rustle of sound he heard, that they should have checked the lean-to room beyond the far door. A board creaked, audible to them all. The plank door swung open.

As he twisted about, bringing his gun around, Trav met a sight almost as startling as if Jack Hinton himself had emerged.

In the doorway stood a girl with her chin lifted defiantly, her wide blue eyes clouded with dread, and with a brown hand pressed tensely below the base of her throat where her

11

gingham began to swell firmly into the rounded womanly form of her bodice. As Trav and Rotan stared at her, she hurried past them, circling as far out as she could go, and came to stand beside the man slumped on the bunk edge.

She placed her other hand on Jenkins' shoulder and faced the intruders.

Jenkins muttered, 'I told you to stay out of sight, Mary.'

'I couldn't stay out after hearing all this,' she said hotly. 'I'll not have you hounded by these—these outlaws!'

Then the small hand that had clutched at her bosom moved unexpectedly. Trav was jolted out of his surprise by a glimpse of what lay concealed within her fingers. She flipped up a small baby derringer. Its muzzle wavered on him, then steadied. He made a threshing headlong dive from his chair as the bullet spat over his head.

His arms struck her, gathered themselves full of cloth and legs, and brought her toppling upon him. Rotan grabbed the tiny weapon as it fell from her grasp. When Trav untangled himself from her and came to his hands and knees, Mary was sprawled on the bare planks fighting down her skirts to cover a high exposure of white flesh. He got to his feet, reached a hand, and in one quick motion hoisted her erect with a lift under her shoulder. Her breasts pumped up and down in

12

her quick breathing. He saw tears of humiliation and frustration form in her dark lashes.

He shot a scowling accusation at Rotan.

'Nothing under that wagon sheet, you said!'

'I just said the fellow didn't have six grown sons,' Rotan replied, turning his palms out. 'How'd I know he would have a daughter in the wagonbed?'

'Miss, I'm sorry I had to butt you over like a mad steer, but you oughtn't to have done that. Those little toy guns could hurt a man.'

The gathering tears slid all the way down her brown pinched cheeks. On the bunk, where he had not moved, Jenkins said, 'This is my daughter. I'm just asking that you don't harm her.'

'Another stunt like that and she'll find herself tied hand and foot and propped in a corner,' Trav said. 'I'm sick of contending with brave people. Now pour that coffee, Rotan. Pour four of 'em, and get the bacon to browning. Miss Jenkins, could I bother you for a clean rag? I seem to have a little bleeding in my leg.'

She blinked puzzledly. 'The bullet? Did I—?'

'You sure did,' Trav lied affably. 'You shot me right through the leg.'

Rotan rumbled over his shoulder, 'They make 'em blood-thirsty up here on the Brazos. Bloodthirsty, but pretty. How you want your sowbelly, Miss? Burnt or greasy?' Mary

13

Jenkins let her appraisal go over Rotan with distaste. 'None at all, thank you. Something has taken my appetite.'

'Let's not any of us get huffy, now,' Trav said patiently. 'We're likely to be chumming up here for a spell. Your father, he's got quite a bit of talking to do. Now, the clean bandage for my leg, please, Miss.'

CHAPTER TWO

Trav had learned many things from the Tonkawas. The tattooed Tonks knew how to wait.

He waited while Jenkins stewed in his own inner turmoil. The girl was not so easy to ignore. There had been feeling in that tumble with her on the floor, bodily impact and bodily revelation, for all its panicky threshings.

As for the man, Trav chose to give Jenkins' mind time to coil rope, thinking it out. Jenkins, watching him and Rotan wolfishly eat, would be a worried homesteader with a hard load to haul this morning. Somewhere in the back of his life, Jenkins had the problem of Jack Hinton. And here and now he had the problem of Trav Parker and Rotan on his hands. Another kind of unappetizing worry, that. Two rough strangers had ridden in and taken over, and Jenkins' daughter was in this

14

house, pretty as a wild flower and promising to any hungering man's eyes and ideas.

After the edge of his appetite wore off and he was working on his second tin cup of coffee, Trav turned once to the silent pair, father and daughter. It was time to prod the man a little.

'While you're thinking, Jenkins, just remember that you're facing a man who's lost sixty thousand dollars, been a prisoner of the Tonkawas, disgraced among the people he used to know, and a long time going hungry while he's trailed Jack Hinton. Let that give you some kind of an idea of what you're up against.'

His glance raked back across Mary as he spoke. Color stained her pinched cheeks. He got busy with his coffee again.

It went against the grain, down deep. Damn it, did she think he enjoyed twisting the knife in her old man? From the dirty clothes and bearded faces of Rotan and himself, she'd be bound to think that they were two bad ones, the scum of the wild land, and that this dirty business was to his liking. An intuition he could not define kept up a tiny pecking far back in his brain. This man and girl were worried about something that roamed a great distance farther off than was visible here.

Rotan kicked his foot under the table.

'Come to, boy!'

Trav bristled. 'You ought to shave. Your table manners could be better, too.'

Rotan dragged a sleeve across his whiskers. His reddened eyes took on a hurt expression.

Trav pushed back. He nervously paced the room. If only the girl didn't look so forlorn. If she just wouldn't keep her hand on Jenkins' big fist as if to comfort him and pledge that they were together in this.

'You better look around the place,' he said to Rotan. 'Don't miss anything.'

Rotan lifted his rifle and lumbered to the door. 'Yeah. Don't you miss anything either, on account of calico gettin' in your eyes!'

When he was gone, Trav faced back to the Jenkins pair.

Jenkins asked dully: 'Are you—Travis Parker?'

Trav made a crooked smile and let it fade off. He tasted the bitter weed behind it. 'The south breeze blows dirt a long way, doesn't it?'

'It does.'

'Well, it blows both ways, Jenkins.'

'I've always been afraid of that.'

'I first heard of you in a saloon in Abilene. You and the others vanished real good after Hinton shot me up.'

Jenkins pulled his hand away from Mary's and rubbed his knuckles, looking down at them. 'I can't get over that man laying for me, up there in the brush. I didn't think they would do that.'

Trav whirled on him. 'Where's Hinton? Where is he, Jenkins?'

16

Jenkins kept cracking his knuckles. He said nodding for a long time. Then, 'The other man, who's he?'

'He's Rotan.'

'I don't like his looks.'

'You won't like mine, either, before I'm through. Let me give you an idea, mister. When I didn't come back from Kansas with John Bradshaw's money from his herd sale, Bradshaw was a ruined man. Everything he'd worked for all his life just disappeared. He was too old to start again. He went out on the plains where just he and God would meet and took his own life. Shot himself through the head with a forty-five. This gun here. Right here in my holster.' He touched the butt of the Colt. 'I thought it would he proper for the same gun to do to Jack Hinton what it did to the man Hinton ruined. Rotan had been Bradshaw's wrangler. When there was no Bradshaw cattle range any more, old Rotan decided to side me on my hunt for Hinton. We're going to get it out of you, mister, one way or the other. And I'm not in a frame of mind to pussyfoot with you all day.'

Mary Jenkins spoke fiercely. 'My father had nothing to do with that robbery!'

'All I'm asking,' Trav replied patiently, 'is where to find Jack Hinton.'

'But that isn't all!' Her proud eyes gave way to pleading. 'It's important to Father—to us—for you to understand that he wasn't in on the

17

robbery. Does that have to plague us all our lives?'

'Don't talk, Mary!' Jenkins said sternly. 'Parker, I'm interested in seeing who it was up there that tried to bushwhack me. Would you take me out to look at him?'

'After Rotan comes back. You made any particular decisions yet?'

Jenkins stared at him, and at something beyond, something far away from the room and beyond the present. He stared that way for a long time. Once, Trav thought he saw grudging surrender form in the man's troubled eyes. But at the last, Jenkins' chin sagged and he rubbed hard on his calloused hands. 'I reckon I don't know where Hinton might be,' he mumbled. 'I could tell you Kansas, Colorado, South Texas, anywhere. You wouldn't know the difference.'

'Don't fool yourself on what I might know and might not. That could cost you. You knew my name. So you ought to know I can get the truth out of a man.'

Jenkins tried to bluster, but it trailed off weakly. 'I don't know anything about Hinton.'

'You don't know anything about telling a convincing lie, that's certain. Did you ever see the Tonks work on a captured Comanche?'

Mary stiffened. 'You wouldn't do that!'

He guessed he was a poor liar, too. She made everything more difficult. After a silent minute, Trav said, 'Let me tell you an item or

18

two that I know about, Jenkins. Maybe this will help you.'

He noticed interest, or speculation, come to Jenkins' face.

'I know, for instance, that Jack Hinton was the only man who could have found out that I was headed south with the herd money from the Abilene buyer. The bank would have told him that, because they had orders to pay it over to me instead of Hinton. He had bossed the herd crew, coming up. But old man Bradshaw didn't trust him on the money end of the deal. There was a fortune, a man's lifetime, involved in this. Bradshaw sent me north to bring back the cash. I never saw Hinton and he didn't know me. But he could have known somebody was taking that money back to Texas. I rode across the Territory alone, and I can tell you it's big and empty, to a man riding alone. You can't sleep with your eyes open nights on end. So this trail boss, Jack Hinton, knew that I had big money on me. I also know that four men rode out of Abilene with Hinton. I've hunted for trace of them everywhere. Three just plain vanished. Maybe Hinton killed them. I don't know. But one, one named Gus Jenkins, finally settled on a homestead above the Cap Rock, up at the tip of the North Fork of the Brazos. I was months finding out even that much.

'So I've found you, Jenkins. The fact that you're alive means to me that Hinton either bribed you, or he's got you bluffed off from talking. I'll find out about that, too, before I'm through. Either way, you probably know where Hinton went with the sixty thousand, what he's doing, what name he's going under. I'll make you talk, if I have to. I know the ways to do it. You should be able to see that this is my life's job. They don't speak to me down there, where I came from, where I used to have friends.' He motioned southward. 'Bradshaw's dead, his family's whipped, and half the people think maybe I just made up the robbery story. There's something else, good and dirty, but I'm not going into it. Not now. Let it sink in, man—you're in mighty big trouble.'

They had followed his words avidly, but at the end, Jenkins sagged even more dejectedly. He said as if to himself, 'Yes, mighty big trouble.'

Rotan came in. 'Looks clear everywhere. He talked yet?'

'He's thinking, at this stage. He asked to see his bushwhacker. You want to walk him up to the brush and see if he knows the man?'

'Come on, nester.' Rotan motioned with the rifle. 'Keep ahead of me. If you jump sudden I'm a sonofabitch if I don't put a slug through your ankle.'

At the door, Jenkins turned. He looked meaningfully at Mary and then at Trav. 'Don't bother my daughter, Parker,' he said with icy vehemence. 'That's the one thing you'd have to kill me about.'

Trav felt his ears burn. 'You don't have to tell me that.'

When they were left alone in the room, he said painfully, 'Rotan talks a little rough.'

Mary stood and asked quietly, 'Is it all right if I start cleaning the kitchen?'

'You got any more little derringers hidden on you?'

'There was only that one.'

'One was plenty.'

'My father made me carry it, always. In case I was about to be captured by Indians.'

'Do I look like a Comanche?'

'No. It was all just—so frightening.'

'That was the biggest little gun I ever saw.'

'I'm sorry. Sorry I shot you.'

'Well, I'm sorry about the wrestle. It was undignified. But interesting while it lasted.'

He held his face expressionless. He saw the color tint her olive skin where the small sun freckles showed.

'You don't look like a bad man.'

'Two ugly strays busted in on you. You had a right to come out shootin'. The bullet didn't hurt much.'

'Excuse me, please.'

She moved past him, no nearer than she could help. She started clearing the dishes.

Back to him, she spoke hesitantly.

'I think I can understand you. A little, anyway. If it's been hard for you, Mr. Parker, remember that it's been bad for us, too. But my father had nothing to do with that holdup. All we want is to be left alone. But I—well, I can feel sorry about all the trouble it's made for you—for those people—the poor man who shot himself. It was a bad thing.'

'Do you know Jack Hinton?'

He saw a slight lifting of her shoulders, shrugging a refusal. Well, he wouldn't badger her. Jenkins would talk. A man couldn't hold out forever. And if he tried to, there were ways to change his mind.

He watched Mary as she worked, and could not remember when he had last been in such a scene—a young woman busy at her kitchen chores. There was a homey quality about it that he liked. This last year, he and Rotan had lived in the brush more often than inside a house, living off the land, bumming when they could, stealing when they had to, going without in between. Before that, there had been his nightmare—like months in the Tonkawa village in the Territory wilds. The ugly squaws at the cook fires, roasting cibolo meat and the smell of it filling the *wetsoxan* lodges, were nothing like this scene in a nester cabin.

He could distinguish the born pride in Mary Jenkins. Put her in dress-up store clothes and walk her out on Sunday among the people in the plaza of Santone, and she would make all the citified heads turn. He read quality in the slanting rise of her cheek bones and proud throat lines, and in the tidy way she went at the kitchen mess Rotan had made. She kept her lips firm, too, even though her misty eyes showed she could do with a good cry.

'Your father,' he said. 'Is he running cattle up here?'

'We have a herd, yes.'

'These last four days, while we were watching your place, you been on a trip somewhere?'

'We only went in for supplies. To Brazos Pass. It's a hard trip in the wagon. We got in early this morning.'

'I know. Rotan was watching.'

'You were watching for us? From the brush?'

'In that deserted shack across the dry creek. I had to hole up somewhere while my leg healed.'

'Your leg wound?'

'I'd lost a little blood.'

'Then I didn't shoot you, after all!'

He had forgotten. He grinned and shook his head. 'I guess I was a little loose with the truth on that. Your bullet went high. When I dived at you the blood seepage started again.'

She turned back to the soapy water in the chipped granite pan. 'We heard about a shooting while we were in Brazos Pass. Two men tried to break into the store one night. They got away.'

'That so? Maybe they were hungry. An

empty stomach might make a man do that.'

'In the settlement, they thought one of them might have been wounded by somebody with a rifle.'

'Could have been. Me, now, I got this nick in my leg crossing the river. A Brazos gar bit me.'

He felt good, hearing her low tinkling laugh. It almost seemed to make them out to be two old friends, having an easy chat while he visited her.

'What's Brazos Pass like?' he asked. 'In daytime, that is.'

Her hoarse, impassioned reply surprised him.

'I hate it—day or night!'

He tried to think quickly how to draw her out on that. 'The settlement itself, or the people?'

The fantasy of a friendly chat with an old friend shattered abruptly. Suspicion and distrust thinned her voice. 'Please. I don't want to talk with you any more.'

They heard footsteps outside. Jenkins came in with Rotan lumbering after him.

'He wants to do a little talking now,' Rotan said without ado. His reddened eyes held Trav with a message. 'What he saw up there decided him.'

Jenkins sank to the bunk edge and nervously massaged his knuckles. 'That man up there was here to get me, no doubt of that.'

24

The nester spoke in a low weary tone. 'I guess this is the end of the trail, for us.'

'Hinton is after you? Is that it?'

'The man you killed—he was Ace Eckhart. He was hired to kill me. You ask where to find Hinton? Well, I'll tell you. I'll tell you something more than that.'

The girl pressed her slender back against the kitchen shelf. Her gaze fastened compassionately upon her father. The April wind clawed over the clapboards outside and the windmill wheel whirled and sent out crazy screechings. Rotan shifted his stance, breathing heavily. Trav stood rigidly before the nester.

He waited, and then quietly prompted Jenkins through dry lips. 'Yes, go on. That's what I want to know.'

'I've got nothing to lose now.' Jenkins seemed to be convincing himself. 'It just means that Mary and I have got to travel again. Pack up and take out.'

Her low voice came across the room. 'It's all right, Father. It had to happen sometime.'

Jenkins hesitated.

Feeling that this was like tediously pushing a heavy boulder uphill, feeling that he had labored it to a delicate balance, Trav again steered Jenkins back to what he had to say.

'So Hinton is—where? Where will I find him, Jenkins?'

Jenkins worked his throat and Trav heard

25

the words begin to form. But they never came out.

To the ears of them all in the quiet room, above the screechy singing of the windmill, there came the far-off drumming sounds of running horses. Jenkins stopped whatever he was about to say. Trav stepped across and picked up the rifle. Rotan lifted Jenkins' gun. The sounds grew to a loud hoof clatter, sweeping into the yard.

A loud yell came. 'Jenkins! Hello, inside!'

Trav motioned. 'Open the door a little and face them, Jenkins. Act natural.'

As he and Rotan covered Jenkins, staying out of sight, the nester opened the door. Through the crack, Trav saw two riders just beyond the porch.

'Indians coming, Jenkins!' one of them shouted. 'They're already across Salt Flat. Get a move on, now!'

The other rider said, 'Better head for Brazos Pass. You and your daughter can make it if you light out fast.'

'All right,' Jenkins said. 'We'll light out.'

'Don't fool around!' the other man warned. 'It's a big bunch. We're going on, now. See you in the settlement.'

His companion yelled back, 'We'll warn the Drains on our way in.'

They kicked their mustangs into a run and were gone.

Trav grasped Jenkins' shoulder and swung

26

him about. 'You were about to say—'

'We've got to run for it!' Jenkins protested. 'Fast!'

'Please!' Mary cried. 'Let's hurry!'

Rotan agreed. 'Come on, Trav! I don't like Comanches to contend with, especially with a female on our hands. Jenkins will keep.'

He understood the urgency in them all, and shared it. He deliberated for seconds, and found himself looking at Mary. 'All right. Saddle up, Jenkins. Don't try any tricks on the ride.'

Jenkins ran for the horse pen. Mary hurried to the lean-to room and returned quickly, dressed in faded riding pants and a frazzled brush jacket. Rotan stuffed cold rations in a sack. Outside, Trav sized up the overcast sky. The windmill slowed, jumped up speed again and raced wildly with a mocking screeching like a mad squaw. The sun was a weak yellow splotch, all but lost in the haze. The land, everywhere, looked chilled to the marrow and lonely.

CHAPTER THREE

There was little time for talk on the punishing ride, and no spare breath for it. Jenkins warned that the race might be nip-and-tuck on getting to the settlement before the Indian

27

party cut them off. The two men who had brought the warning were from the next homestead outfit, he said, five miles east. The drifting dust of this pair could be sighted to the north.

'They'll circle to warn the Drains,' Jenkins said. 'That's the only other family this side of Brazos Pass.'

Trav and Rotan ate dust. They permitted the girl to set the speed with her long-haired Spanish pony. To himself, Trav cursed the interruption. The raid threat had silenced the nester just when the answer on Jack Hinton had seemed to be forming. But he had raked in at least a part of the big stakes. He had found the man who knew. The rest he would dig out of Jenkins at the end of the ride.

When the horses could no longer hold to the fast gait, they pulled them down from their unsteady lope and walked them for a time through gully-slashed plains.

Jenkins gestured. 'No dust behind us. I hope everybody got out. The Indians could be a tame bunch, coming to trade at Brazos Pass. Or they could be fired up to try for some captives and horses. Never know, so it's smarter to run.'

'Why do you live in such a country?' Trav asked.

'Grass.'

'Yes, but is it worth it, having the Indians to contend with ever so often?'

'Texas ought to give us a little help,' Jenkins complained. 'They ought to send some Rangers.'

'You think the state should do that, eh?'

'Down at Austin they don't even know what's up here.'

'Yes, they should send you some Rangers,' Trav remarked. 'They don't have enough now to ride the country where they're really needed. So headquarters should send a company up here to wet nurse a scattering of nesters.'

Mary faced back to him. 'That was sarcastic, Mr. Parker. My father is trying to say that this would be fine cattle country, if the state would keep the Indians above the Red River where they're supposed to stay.'

He let that go unanswered. He had spotted dust to the northeast and he called Rotan's attention to it.

'Not a big bunch, whoever it is,' Rotan decided.

'Not over three or four, I'd say.'

Jenkins slowed to study the dust trace. It floated along at an angle that would intercept their own route.

'It could be Lige Drain and his wife,' he said. 'Least I hope that's who it is. They would be coming from that direction.'

Soon the approaching riders were visible. There were three of them. two men and a woman. Jenkins said, 'We'll meet up with them

29

at Owl Bluff. Horses need a rest.'

'Watch your talk now, Jenkins,' Trav warned. 'Don't try anything. The same goes for your daughter. We're somebody you just happened to meet up with, riding this way.'

Jenkins returned Travs hard gaze. 'I've given my word, Parker.'

After a mile, Jenkins reported, 'That's Drain and his wife, all right. Don't know the man with them.'

The two parties met and by silent agreement pulled up to rest their horses. Trav made a quick study of the couple and of the second man. Drain was a hawk-eyed old-timer, and his wife showed the history of many frontier hardships in her facial lines and worn hands. The other man was of a different stripe altogether—aloof, undersized, sporting long sideburns, crooked yellow teeth and a yellow neckerchief. He drifted pale eyes over the three men, and then settled them for a full, appreciative inventory of Mary. Trav took note, as he always did, of the man's saddle rig. It was a flashy hand-tooled job, speaking a man's estimated worth of himself, and the same went for the leather holster with its white-handled Colt. The man chewed a twig, working his thin mouth constantly, and in a moment he spat it aside without once taking his speculation off Mary.

Lige Drain said, 'This is a rider we ran across. Told him the news, so he turned back for Brazos Pass. Name of Cabbo.'

Cabbo flicked a negligent glance to Jenkins, then held it a little longer on Trav and Rotan.

'Started out to join a friend of mine, on a hunt,' Cabbo said tonelessly. 'Somewhere back there.' He motioned. 'I decided to ride back to town after these people told me about the redskins.' He legged off his horse and stood apart from the others.

Drain started to make conversation with Jenkins, but Trav spoke over their words, to Cabbo.

'What was your friend's name?'

'Name?' He played a cold look over Trav.

'Yeah. Name.'

'You're a little inquisitive, stranger.'

Trav nodded. 'Could be. I thought maybe we'd run across him somewhere, back where he was on the hunt.'

Cabbo played his fingers on his gunbelt. 'His name happened to be Ace Eckhart.'

Trav shot a look at Jenkins. The nester went stiff. Cabbo noticed something he did not understand. His voice turned flinty.

'You see anything of him?'

Trav nodded. 'Just happens we did.'

'He was supposed to wait for me. I got started late.'

'Well, he's waiting, I guess.'

Jenkins spoke painfully. 'You're new out here, I take it.'

'Tolerably so.' Cabbo's eyes half-closed. He

31

spoke softly to Trav. 'Your name don't happen to be Jenkins, does it?'

'Happens not, friend.'

'Where was this you saw Ace? What was he doing?'

'Hunting. Like you said.'

He saw Cabbo's eyes go dead. 'I just asked you.'

'Eckhart was taking a nap when I saw him last.'

Cabbo stood unmoving. Then he turned and stared at Gus Jenkins as if discovering him there for the first time. After a long moment he mounted, swung his horse about, and said flatly, 'I'll see you in town.' His last lingering gaze was for Trav, and then he hit with the spurs and was off at a pounding gallop.

Drain murmured, 'I don't know the man, but I can take an oath I don't like his looks. Glad he's left us.'

'And I didn't like his manners, the way he stared at Mary,' his wife added.

'I wish you two would think back a minute,' Trav said. 'Riding up, after you could see who we were—did you call any name? Did you mention Jenkins here?'

They shook their heads. 'I just mentioned you were some more people running for the settlement,' Drain said. 'Why?'

'Just wondered.'

Mrs. Drain repeated the complaint that Jenkins and his daughter had made earlier.

32

'You'd think the Rangers would come stop these raids! I'll declare, Texas just lets the redskins run wild up here. Driving off our cattle, killing any of us they can catch, or worse.'

'Austin doesn't care,' her husband said. 'We're five hundred miles out of their thoughts.'

That's a sore subject with these nesters, Trav told himself. He caught a lowered movement of Rotan's bushy brow and frowned back.

'Mr. Parker here says they don't have enough men,' Mary remarked.

'They'd have enough if they weren't sittin' around those South Texas towns doing nothing.'

Rotan coughed. 'Maybe the Rangers don't know there're any Texans up here this side of the Brazos. Maybe they never bothered to look at a map.'

'They could give us some protection if they wanted to,' Drain rumbled.

'I don't think they're just sitting around,' Trav said mildly. 'For instance, Company B is patrolling the whole border from Brownsville to El Paso. They've got Company C strung up and down the Pecos because not all the Comanches are out of that country down there. Captain Small has a garrison working out of Fort Belknap. The others are scattered all over. Always too few in too big a country.'

33

Mrs. Drain regarded him with interest. 'You seem to know a lot about them. Are you just recent out of the south part?'

'Yes, ma'am. Just recent.'

Drain said, 'Looks to me like the judge would have enough influence by now to get us some protection up here. He can do everything else he pleases.'

Something made Trav work a veiled glance from one to the other in the silent moment that followed. He wondered what hidden play of meaning seemed to be going among them. Then he dismissed it as imagination. Keeping their attention on the eastern horizon, they brought their talk back to the present Indian scare.

But Rotan's attention had been flagged, too. He came back to it in a moment. 'Who's this judge you mentioned?'

Drain grunted, 'Man, you *are* new up here.'

'He just runs Brazos Pass and everything in this whole country,' Mrs. Drain said affably. 'The judge is a fine man, though.'

'You ought to see Wilda, his wife,' Drain said.

Mrs. Drain bristled. 'Lige!'

Jenkins spoke sharply. 'Let's get movin'.'

In the afternoon, with their horses dragging from the pace, they came over a rolling ridge and sighted the settlement of Brazos Pass.

Visible to the northeast, the zigzag line of a chalky ravine marked the northernmost trickle of the Brazos River. On the other side of the settlement, broad miles of grass suggested a gigantic green blanket with its western edges in eternity.

'Hey,' Drain said, addressing Jenkins, 'you hear about the shooting not long ago? Couple of bandits tried to rob the store. Got away, but one left blood traces.'

'And it was a good thing they didn't get caught,' Mrs. Drain added. 'I'll bet the judge would have had that fellow Raffer slice their ears off.'

Mary murmured, 'Yes, we heard about it.' She averted her eyes from Trav.

'Who's Raffer?' Rotan asked.

'The judge's gun!' Drain retorted. 'The judge made himself judge in the first place, then made Raffer his town marshal. Raffer could shoot their ears off. He can do anything with a sixgun that most men can do with a knife.'

When the distance to the settlement closed to a mile, Trav spurred alongside Jenkins. 'Let the others go in. We need to talk over that business before we get into the town.'

The Drains looked curiously at them, but Jenkins nodded tight-lipped and motioned them on. 'We'll be in a little later.'

'Uh-oh!' Rotan abruptly pointed. 'I reckon we're all goin' in, and pronto! Look comin'!'

The others saw it almost at the same time. Up from the distant ravine that fed into the cut of the Brazos, colored specks of movement came boiling out of its scarred ridges like red ants.

The band rode slowly, with their paint already throwing glistening colors against the sunlight. They came down the ridges, straggled on a widening front and rode steadily toward the village. Trav counted a few of the moving dots and then guessed the force to number more than a hundred.

'That's a war party,' Rotan said. 'They've got rifles.'

'They're not after your cattle this time,' Trav said, studying the oncoming formation. 'They're headed for a bigger haul, or else a trading visit. I wouldn't gamble which. That town had better be set for trouble.'

'It'll be set,' Jenkins replied.

They urged the mustangs into a run down the last slope of prairie and into the settlement.

The other time, in this town, when Trav had received the bullet wound in his leg from some sharpshooter's probing of a sound in the night, and when he and Rotan had ridden out ahead of the chase, darkness had concealed the little settlement. Now he saw Brazos Pass exposed in the afternoon light with all its drab skeleton showing. Whoever the first man was, staking off a townsite here at the top of the Brazos, he had been either optimistic or a fool, Trav thought. North and west there was nobody.

East a way was the Territory. Southward was the rest of Texas with a three-hundred-mile gap between it and this Cap Rock outpost. But it was a town, of sorts.

He looked it over with interest as they came to the foot of the one sandy street. At the far end, in a stunty grove of blackjack oaks, stood the long adobe shape of the main store, the place where he and Rotan had tried to restock their ration bags with near disastrous results. Across the road at an angle, another building of some size sported a sign, THE BRAZOS PALACE. He also saw the wagon yard with its barn and windmill, horse pens, a blacksmith shop, and counted a dozen houses.

A man who appeared to be posted for that purpose came to meet them, running his horse.

He wasted no time in formalities. 'Jenkins, Drain, you other fellows, head for Kamack's house, yonder on the east edge.' He pointed. 'That's where we're weak. The judge has posted rifles enough along here, and in the houses on the north side. If they circle and hit from the west, you men at Kamack's move fast to reinforce us over there. Main thing, be ready if they charge.'

He whirled his horse and raced north on the weedy street. Mrs. Drain and Mary followed him. The four men headed for the squat stone house east of the road a quarter of a mile. They hurriedly tied their horses in the

37

mesquite saplings. A gaunt man opened the door and motioned them in.

'Pick you a window and keep your noggins down when they get in range. Them bullies have got rifles, same as us, Territory law notwithstanding.'

A dead voice came across the gloom. 'Well, the nester bastard showed up.'

The room went graveyard quiet.

Somebody said, 'Who's a nester bastard, Cabbo?'

'Him. The one name of Jenkins. Why didn't you bring the good-lookin' filly in? It'd be nice to be cooped up with her tonight.'

In the gloom, Trav heard Jenkins' breath flow out as if he had been hit. Trav pushed by Kamack, who had been interrupted in giving instructions. He stopped two feet from the slack figure of Cabbo. Somewhere behind him he heard Jenkins mumble, 'No, be careful, Parker,' but the warning glanced off the ringing anger in him. If the pale-eyed man thought that Trav would start with conversation, his mistake quickly became apparent. A killer had to be dealt with fast. Cabbo had to be given the brutal trick. The Tonks had taught Trav many things.

While Cabbo still fondled his gun butt, Trav kicked high in a fixed aim with his good right leg. In a fleshy thud, his hard boot instep caught Cabbo low under the gunbelt. Cabbo cried out in his throat and bent low with his palms spread to his pain. Trav measured, and with the timing of unbroken rhythm he swung his boot again. The toe cracked exactly against the bone of Cabbo's chin. He reeled backward. Trav glided after him. He slapped Cabbo hard with his open hand, his right and then his left. He whispered, 'That's for the girl,' and when Cabbo was exposed properly he delivered a fist from his hip into Cabbo's yellow throat scarf. The man went down kicking and gagging against the wall.

Painfully, because his leg wound hurt him now and his knuckles felt cracked, Trav tried to throw off the two men who powered in to grab him. Another man pushed between him and Cabbo. Kamack yelled, 'Stop it! Stop it!'

One of the men bulldogging Trav's right arm muttered, 'You tryin' to get yourself shot?'

Rotan shouldered aside the man standing over Cabbo. He nursed his heavy Colt in one fist, and with his other hand he twisted Cabbo's gun from its holster.

Somebody remarked, 'Cabbo and Raffer ain't goin' to like this feller.'

'Man those windows!' Kamack ordered. 'Here they come!'

Trav fought off the restraining arms. He joined a man at a front window and made a quick study of the approaching procession. The Indians were no more than half a mile out now. He took in the straggled formation which had changed to a winding file. This snaked back from its leader, a stiff-riding figure in chieftain's trappings with his legs dangling from his spotted *mesteno*. Trav strained his gaze in disbelief and felt his muscles go rigid. Then he started for the door.

'This doesn't have to be a fight, if it's handled right!'

He unbarred the door and stepped outside.

'Hey, get back in here and shut that door!'

'Those Comanches will chew you up!' somebody warned.

'Those are no Comanches,' he retorted, watching the file.

Kamack called, 'Not Comanches?'

'No. Tonkawas. That's Blue Knife leading them.'

'You mean you know that bunch?'

'Know 'em, hell!' Rotan cut in. 'He's practically kin folks with 'em!'

Trav limped across the yard. 'Cover me,' he called. 'But I don't want a shot fired unless they start it.' By the time he had mounted, Rotan came jogging up. Trav stopped. 'I'd rather you kept your eyes peeled on Cabbo. I don't want to get shot in the back. You're responsible for Jenkins, too.'

Rotan dropped behind, muttering protest. Trav walked his horse. The leading rider of the strung-out file of Indians had sighted this movement. The chief pulled up his horse and the painted procession behind him came to a ragged halt.

40

As he rode out of the yard, Trav heard an excited voice back at the doorway. 'Look yonder—the judge is riding out to palaver with 'em, too. Going right out to meet 'em, same as Parker.'

Turning, Trav saw a black-garbed giant on a massive red horse approaching from his left. The judge was coming from the far north end of the street. They neared from converging angles and came within speaking distance of the painted chief at about the same time, but Trav made the first sign.

He rubbed his hand across his right ribs, where the old Territory ambush wound had left its scar, and then lifted his fingers in the friendship sign of the Tonkawas.

'Blue Knife has roamed far from his home fires,' he said. 'He has crossed the Brazos and found a white brother. Blue Knife is looking at Death-In-The-Ribs. Remember?'

CHAPTER FOUR

The old Tonkawa was as inscrutable now as he had been in the days when this white man was his prisoner, languishing within a small whisper of death. Seeing the crusty old warrior made time race backward for Trav. Here out of thin air was a living symbol of all that had happened, of the start of his long search, and

41

the many hazy trails that had led him to this strange afternoon in Brazos Pass. For a moment the present fell away. The restless rifle-armed warriors beyond Blue Knife floated into old recognitions and some became faces and names and incidents recalled from the past.

But he watched Blue Knife. He saw the web of wrinkles begin to mesh beneath the circular smears of box-elder paint.

'Blue Knife remembers. He is looking at Death-In-The-Ribs. This is not good. The white man who became a friend of my village does not belong with the evil ones here who send the Comanche wolves against us.'

'I am not one of these in the settlement,' Trav said.

'The head paleface here speaks with two tongues—one to the Comanches, one to the white chiefs of the Territory.'

Trav tried to digest Blue Knife's meaning. He couldn't make anything out of it.

A harsh voice broke in. 'I'll take over here. What does the old hyena want?'

Trav pulled his attention from Blue Knife. For the first time, he looked at the giant who had come up beside him. He saw a powerfully welded, confident man of about forty whose set scowl showed contempt for this Indian, or for any man of any color who might get in his way. The judge's thick and weathered jaw jutted from a bull neck to top off his hard and

42

serviceable build. He kept a thick finger curled to the trigger of the Winchester across his red California saddle. But incongruously, he wore a half-wilted little decoration of bluebonnet blossoms poked through a lapel slit in his black calfhide jacket. His studied arrogance rubbed Trav's raw nerve edges, causing him to grin maliciously through his dirt-crusted stubble.

'They're apt to pluck that bouquet off of you, judge. And a few other of your decorations.'

'My wife wouldn't like that, in either case. But I'll handle this.'

'All right. You're the big Brazos Pass ramrod. Here's a crate of rattlesnakes for you to play with.'

The stabbing black eyes lost none of their hardness, but the lumpy corners of the judge's mouth made a mocking curl under a careless mustache line. Some inner tasting of the situation seemed to touch a chord of irony in him.

'Everybody in the houses behind us is bleeding goose pimples,' he said, 'but you came barrelin' out here like it was a free day in a bawdy house. I don't savvy you. What does this old boy want?'

'You were taking over,' Trav reminded him.

'I was and have. Now I'm asking you questions. Who are you?'

'We'll take 'em one at a time,' Trav said. 'Who I am is my business. What this crowd wants I haven't found out yet. This one here is Blue Knife and if you want to keep all your decorations don't start off thinking he's not as smart as you are. They're Tonkawas.'

'Stinkin' cannibals!'

'That's never been proved,' Trav said. 'But cannibals or not, you've got 'em at your back door and I can tell you Blue Knife is beginning to feel the redskin's insult right now because you're palavering with me and not with him. You want me to find out what they're after, or have you taken over like you said?'

'What was it he told you?'

'Something they don't like about your town. Something about trading with the Comanches. Any light on that?'

The judge hesitated. 'We do a little trading.'

'Well, maybe you can put it together better than I can. It's big to them, else they wouldn't have ridden this far to tell you so.'

The judge gestured. 'He's your cousin. Keep making talk.'

In a long, tedious harangue, using the hand signs and as many Tonkawa words as he could remember, Trav made talk with Blue Knife. Twenty yards beyond them the painted warriors waited uneasily.

Trav turned back to the judge.

'The Tonkawas and Comanches have been enemies since the Day One, as you may know. Blue Knife is saying that somebody here trades guns and whiskey to the Comanches for stolen

44

trail beef. What he didn't say in so many words, but means, is that the Comanches have damn near chastized the Tonks back to the last little corner of the Territory. This is a washed-up tribe but they're making a last-ditch fight out of it. They're mad at Brazos Pass and I think they'd like to go down with one last good battle under their belts.'

The judge gestured impatiently. 'You tell him this.' He moved the rifle in a menacing swing. 'You tell him to get his goddam cannibal crew off this prairie in five minutes or he'll have to drag 'em home dead! Tell him there's a whole army of rifles behind us—'

Blue Knife stiffened. Trav said, 'Don't be a fool, judge!'

'You tell him—'

'He understands English, man!'

Blue Knife jerked his mustang around. He shot up his fist in a quick, angry signal.

Trav gritted, 'Look out, now, judge! You've started trouble you didn't have to start!'

Blue Knife jabbered at Trav.

'They want you, judge. They'll just take you as hostage until this thing is settled.'

'Like hell they will!'

Trav tried to placate Blue Knife, calling across the short distance. But the chief ignored him now. He made an angry motion, and wound up pointing a long naked arm at the judge. Behind him the Tonkawa bucks kicked their ponies into motion and whipped up their

45

rifles. In that delicate moment, while Trav racked his brain for the right words to halt the chiefs evident intention, the whole silent world seemed to shake apart with the sound of a gun shot behind him. The explosion boomed out from Kamack's house. Trav cursed somebody unknown and watched Blue Knife.

In that short second of indecision, two more shots sounded, close together.

Strangely, Trav listened for the whine of bullets without hearing it, and could conceive of no reason why the defenders in the house would fire on the powwow while he and the judge were helplessly exposed.

But the gun blasts settled the issue for the Tonkawas. As if those explosions had ended all their uncertainty, the warriors broke out in a high gobble of words. The mass of ponies churned, and then a reckless segment of young bucks yelled their mounts into a confused charge upon the white men.

A quick sidewise glance showed Trav that the judge's face had paled. The judge jabbed the rifle butt to his heavy shoulder. Trav plunged his horse headlong at the big red and blindly smashed his fist down on the judge's rifle barrel.

'You damn fool!'

Then the Indians were upon them. The Tonks plunged in, barking like a pen of wounded coyotes, flourishing their guns and knives. Trav shouted, trying to stem their

46

crowded advance upon the judge. He called the names that went with faces he remembered, and orders to them in their own tongue. In this confusion of colliding horses and choking dust, the bucks milled past him. The melee engulfed the big red horse. Trav fought his spooked mustang and forced his way into the middle of the confusion by clubbing the heads of the Indian horses. A warrior called, 'Death-In-TheRibs!' Somewhere in the mixup the judge's voice croaked, 'Call 'em off! Call 'em off of me!' When Trav finally fought his mustang through the mass, he saw that the big man's face was scratched and bleeding. His clothes had been ripped and his rifle lay in the dirt.

The judge tried to turn his horse and power his way out. The movement set off yells. As if this little taste of battle had touched off a hysteria for greater action, the Tonkawas yelled triumphantly and closed in again. Like a dog pack playing with a wounded fox, they trapped the judge again in the weight of their numbers. The big red reared and squealed from a vicious knife jab in the rump. A long, paint-circled arm shot aloft among the milling bodies. Trav saw a glistening knife blade.

'Fire Feather!' he yelled.

He spurred his horse at the Tonkawa. Straining, he reached the uplifted wrist. He twisted savagely. The blade dropped to earth. He kicked outward with his stirrup and heard

Fire Feather's yelp of pain as the stirrup grated on bone.

A kid warrior tore the judge's reins from his hand. Now the big man had to hold on to his saddle-horn, and in his naked admission of helplessness he twisted his neck, searching for Trav in silent appeal. The buck with the reins jerked the red horse forward and the others closed in. The judge was being led, surrounded, by triumphantly barking captors.

Into this mass that momentarily had cut him off, Trav once more forced his mustang, plunging the animal into the confusion, and made it to the judge's side. Repeatedly, he called the names of those he remembered, and they grudgingly gave ground to him. Finally, he tore the reins from the hand of the man controlling the judge's horse and blocked the procession to a halt.

'Don't move! Don't say anything!' Trav snarled at the big man. 'You'll hold your damned tongue now or lose it for keeps!'

He stretched high in his stirrups. 'Fall back! Fall back, brothers! Blue Knife is your great chief. Death-In-The-Ribs will talk with Blue Knife.' They hesitated. He clinched their attention by tearing back his brush jacket and shirt. He twisted in the saddle, facing them, holding back his clothes from his exposed body and showing them the long red welt of the flesh scar where the bullet of death had been dug out by their own medicine men.

Blue Knife rode close to him. Trav said, 'Those shots were not fired at your warriors. The town wishes to be friends with Blue Knife's people. The Tonkawas need trade goods. This you will get if you wait. You will get nothing if you take the white chief.' He indicated the grim-faced judge. 'Death-In-The-Ribs gives you his blood promise—release the white chief to me and you will get more than the Comanches ever got, to take back to your people!'

Blue Knife thought it over. He spoke with dignity: 'We trust our white brother.'

'All right. We will make trade talk, later. Camp your tribe yonder in the grove. The town will send you meat and tobacco at once.'

In the end it did not take much argument. On the promise of rations and tobacco now, and a trade talk later, Blue Knife called his men into a growling conference that finally trickled out to uneasy silence. Then the band rode slowly southward toward a grove of pin oaks.

The judge flipped a finger of sweat off his jaw. 'Much obliged,' he said.

'Whoever fired those shots back there ought to be quartered and hung.'

'I agree.'

The judge wiped at a bruise on his face. He retrieved his hat and rifle from the ground. Trav watched the big man's painful movements. The judge muttered a string of

49

oaths and finished ripping off the torn fragment of his hatband. But even in the mauling he had taken, the frayed little bunch of blue flowers had stayed intact in his jacket buttonhole.

'For a minute I thought those bastards had me,' he said.

'For a minute,' Trav agreed, 'they damn sure did. You asked for it.'

The judge gathered up his reins.

'I know when my life has been saved by somebody,' he said roughly, not looking at Trav. 'I don't know how you did it but you did.'

'They saved my life, once, that's the reason. They kept me a prisoner a long time because they were just plain curious. They couldn't decide whether I was a live man going around dead or a dead man come back to life. They don't know for sure, even yet.'

'You come with me.' The way he said it, it was an order. 'Whatever you want at the store or the Brazos Palace is yours. I own 'em. I want you to take over when we hold the powwow. I've got to get those cannibals out of here without it costing me any more than possible. You name your price. You're working for me, starting now.'

Trav started to mention that he hadn't been consulted yet about that. But he had another idea. Maybe he could obtain information or help from the judge in his own private mission. He would play it down the line until he figured out a few things. Right now he wanted to get back to Jenkins.

'I'll take you up on that,' he said, 'at least for the time being. I've got a friend in that rock house yonder. We need some clean duds and a place to shave and rest up a little.

'We're a little behind with our eating, too. You furnish us that and I guess we're even.'

'It's done. Get your friend and come on to the Palace. Whiskey first, if you want it when you get there. By the way, when you go by Kamack's place, tell Cliff Cabbo to make the rounds of all my hands and keep 'em on the alert in this Indian business. Nobody sleeps tonight.'

Trav had to freeze his features to hide his surprise. He managed to control his voice.

'Cabbo? Does he work for you?'

'Nearly everybody around here works for me,' the judge said.

'That so?'

'I own the goddam Brazos.'

Watching him, Trav saw the red glints of pride and hungering power burn almost crazily in the judge's challenging eyes. And he thought of the ambush at Gus Jenkins' shack.

'Does Ace Eckhart work for you?'

They were at the edge of the settlement now. The judge said, 'I'm a blunt man. When I hear a question I want to know what's in the mind of the man behind it. Why?'

'Nothing. I just heard Cabbo mention him.'

51

'You rode in with Jenkins, didn't you? Mary said two strangers came in with them.'

'We happened to run across Jenkins and his daughter.'

'Then maybe you happened to run into Ace Eckhart.'

'No. Like I said, Cabbo just mentioned the name. Seems that he hunted for Eckhart somewhere out there and didn't find him.' Then Trav added flatly, 'I don't believe I've heard your name.'

'I'm Denver Smith. They call me the judge.'

'You own the court, like the town?'

'I had me an election and got elected judge without losing a vote. I hold court when I decide it's needed.'

The name meant nothing. The rest of it turned all the cards face up. Denver Smith was saying that he was the czar above the Brazos. A hard man and proud of it, dodging no challenge.

Whatever wispy suspicion had touched the back of his mind now became obscured and Trav put his thoughts to other things. The judge reined away. 'You come to the Palace. Like I said, I owe you whatever you have a mind for. And by the way, I didn't hear your name.'

Trav could tell him truthfully or not. He decided it made no difference.

'Travis Parker.'

He could not tell whether the granite

features changed expression or not. Or did the judge reply too carelessly? 'All right, Parker. Bring your friend. And don't forget to tell Cabbo to carry out his assignment before dark.'

All Trav knew, leaving the judge, was a new form of uneasiness. He felt that he must hurry, and get Jenkins—get the man away, and work on him for his answer.

He found the men at Kamack's bunched outside the doorway and immediately smelled trouble in the uneasy way they watched his approach. Rotan detached himself from the group and ambled forward.

A distance out from the stone house Rotan motioned for him to pull up.

'Who in hell fired those shots?' Trav demanded. 'Did they want to get us scalped right before their eyes?'

'I hate to tell you something, boy. I'd rather break a leg.'

Trav stared down at Rotan's suffering countenance and then dismounted. They faced each other. Rotan stared up painfully at the taller man. Trav waited. What was one more problem? After all the months of bad problems, what did one more matter? He wiped his sleeve across his sanded stubble. Still, he didn't like the older man's haunted expression.

'Go on.'

'It's Jenkins.'

53

'All right, it's Jenkins. What has he done?'

'We lost him, Trav.'

'Tell it to me!'

'You can kick me all over the Cap Rock for the hound dog I feel like. But I lost him for you.'

Trav stepped back and leaned against the saddle skirt. 'Don't make me worry with riddles. I'm tired.'

Rotan scuffed a boot toe in agony. His voice wheezed through his beard, barely audible.

'Cabbo killed Jenkins.'

Trav leaned harder against his horse. The buckskin braced to take his weight. He felt his tiredness clear to the middle of his bones. The rock house and the little knot of men there, the prairie beyond, the far off color of Blue Knife's camp in the grove, all shrank small in the late haze and became buzzing gnats of unreality. A dull throbbing began in his leg. Maybe the judge's store had decent bandage and salve.

Rotan spoke far away. 'Those shots. All at once Cabbo come unglued and grabbed a gun from somebody. He turned it on Jenkins. All of us were watching you out there. Cabbo did this mighty fast. He ran out the back and was nearly gone before I could get a bead on him. But he won't back—shoot nobody else.'

Words choked Trav's gullet. 'Jenkins is dead?'

'He's dead.'

'Did he—could he say *anything*?'

'Not a word.'

Nothing made much difference now. Jenkins was dead, and he had been the only clue. Trav murmured, 'He wasn't a bad man.'

'No. He was doing the best he could. That Ace Eckhart and Cabbo, they were out to get him.'

'Cabbo worked for the judge,' Trav muttered.

'Well, he's as dead as Jenkins, but that ain't much satisfaction.'

'Jack Hinton wanted the nester dead. Isn't that what Jenkins said? Damn it, Cabbo worked for the judge and he sidekicked with Eckhart and he killed Jenkins!'

'Who's this judge?'

'He rules the roost. Name of Denver Smith.'

'This adding up to anything?'

Trav knuckled at the sweat and dirt on his jaw. 'It could be a private feud—or it could mean something else. Damned if I know.'

'We still got the girl.'

'I've thought about that. She knows the same thing Jenkins knew. But forcing it out of her is something different.'

'You'll have to forget she's a girl,' Rotan muttered.

Trav shrugged. 'Somebody will have to tell her about this. Not me. I can't. You get somebody to do that. I don't want to face her yet.'

'A man's already left for that.'

'What'd those men have to say about Jenkins getting shot in the back?'

'They don't talk. Except one mentioned the judge would find that Cabbo did it in self-defense. Funny damn bunch of people.'

'Well, I'm going to that saloon with the fancy name. Get your horse. I'll want to find out about Cabbo, later. Right now, the judge is playing the big host.' He managed a grin through the bitterness he felt. 'We'll get some clothes and grub and maybe a bed out of this. Also maybe a bullet in the back. You want to take a chance or head out of here?'

'We've ridden a long way,' Rotan said. 'Too long to quit.'

'Way I feel. Let's look 'em over. All the cottonmouth moccasins aren't playing in the Brazos. Some came upland and grew two legs. But first, I want some other stuff the big boy's got yonder in the Brazos Palace. Whiskey.'

Rotan headed for his horse. 'Me, too. A bottle apiece, to start.'

CHAPTER FIVE

Before Trav tilted the bottle to the shot glass he spoke cautiously to the bartender. 'These are supposed to be on the house. Did the judge tell you?'

'Your name Parker?'

'That's right.'

'You're the one that plucked him out of that Tonk ruckus?'

'Just say if the drinks are free or not. It'll make a difference in the way they go down.'

'Wait a minute.' The bartender reached with a fleshy paw to stay the bottle. 'You get better stuff than this. Back room.'

Trav looked toward the dimly lighted rear of the long room. The Brazos Palace, contrary to its surroundings, struck him as a fine and fancy place inside. The judge had grandiose ideas, according to the furnishings and trappings. Everything but cash customers.

'Back room it is. Where's the judge?'

'He and Raffer are out seein' that the men keep on the lookout for those Tonks.' The bartender watched Rotan sympathetically. Rotan was taking no chances. This was whiskey in the hand, right here and now, and the back room might fall in, blow up or burn down before he got there. He took over the bottle, sloshed out a glass of the fiery red bar rotgut, whipped his elbow high, locked it. He jerked his shoulders and made a sound in his lungs like a wounded boar. 'That'll do to start. Now where's the back room and the good stuff?'

Trav knew that Rotan was still blaming himself for what had happened to Jenkins. The old-timer needed that whiskey jolt, he admitted as he led the way back through the deserted main room, past the balcony stairway, and down a short hall to an open door. The beaded glass shade of a hanging coal oil lamp bathed yellow tones over a carpet, desk and chairs. Rotan had been morose, riding in. They had stabled their horses in silence before angling across the empty road to the Palace. The townspeople were still keeping to their houses. The settlement might have been a graveyard, for all the life they could see. Even the boy at the stables had been untalkative. Judge Denver Smith's little lost empire was not the happiest metropolis Trav had ever seen and he wondered if it went stoop-shouldered under the same weight when there was no Indian scare. Dusk had settled.

'On the desk.' Trav pointed. 'I guess it's for us. Watch it—the way I feel about the judge the bottle may be wired to a copperhead. Wonder what those desk drawers would show about him? You think I could do any better burglaring them than I did his store the other night?'

'Just burglar the bottle. I want something to take the taste of the other one out of my mouth.'

The whiskey bottle had been uncorked but was full. Two shot glasses stood beside it and Trav poured them level. The whiskey went down clutching and burning, but with a ripe and friendly after warmth to it, and this time

Rotan did not shudder like a shot animal.

Trav deliberated before the second. Rotan prompted him with a jab at his arm. 'Keep workin'. First one just cocked the hammer, now we got to pull the trigger.'

'It's pulled.' Trav slanted the bottle. The whiskey trickled over. A few drops rolled off like shimmering buck-shots across the judge's bare-topped desk. Rotan stabbed their flow with his fingers, then he mopped the stained surface with his ragged sleeve. Trav told himself that it was thinking of the judge's desk drawers that had made his hand unsteady.

He muttered, 'What am I expecting to find out about the judge, anyway?'

Rotan grunted 'Huh?' and when Trav absently shook his head, Rotan said, 'Been a long time since we last done this.' He gulped the drink. His throat made a pleased sound like trying to hold on to the taste velveting the lining. 'Santone, wasn't it?'

'Who remembers that far back?'

They looked away from each other, because the trouble of the moment still hung there between them. Jenkins was dead, and there in an instant had gone a year of searching. A slow and wearisome hunt had played out in a box canyon. It was nothing to talk about now. The whiskey made a good raft to grab for.

'Cliff Cabbo.' Trav sat on the desk edge. 'First Ace Eckhart was after him, then Cabbo. Gus Jenkins' life wasn't worth a tin dollar up

59

here. Wasn't very pleasant for the girl, either.'

'Mary, she's a looker!'

'Is she? I didn't notice.'

'You're a damn liar, Travis Parker. What she had you couldn't of missed.'

It would be a tragic blow for her, Trav thought. She had been intensely loyal to her father. Had to be, to live up here. And there was the way she had come out to protect the old man, uncorking that little derringer from a place he'd least expect a gun to come. He cursed softly, for what Cliff Cabbo had done to him, to Jenkins, and to Mary, and he did this until he had relieved his tension and vented his hatred for Cliff Cabbo even with Cabbo dead.

'We've got to know why!' he said. 'Why did Cabbo kill him?'

'Maybe she would know.'

'Mary?'

'Yeah. If we could get her to talk.'

'I asked her, back at her place, if she knew Jack Hinton.'

'Bet you didn't get a cheep out of her.'

'Not a word. She kept washing dishes like I wasn't there.

They thought of these things for a while, working with their own speculations, and had their third sample of judge Denver Smith's hospitality.

Trav asked then, 'How do you suppose a place like this pays its way, with no more business than it'd have in this country?

60

Nobody lives up here, nobody ever comes this way.

Rotan chuckled. 'Go on. Take a tally of them drawers. I see you're itchin' to.'

The barkeep padded in silently and Trav wondered if he had overheard Rotan's words. The man's sleepy orbs batted in his glistening bald skull. 'There's a room for you gents upstairs. The judge said tell you to go get cleaned up. New duds for you up there, too. If they don't fit I'll take 'em across to the store and trade 'em for some that do. Room's at the left end of the hall. Don't bust into the others by mistake they're the quarters of the judge and his wife.' He gave a quick estimating glance at the bottle, mumbled, 'I'd a thought you was drier than that,' and lumbered out.

Trav studied the front of the desk again. He reached and inched out the top drawer.

'Match the hallway,' he whispered. Rotan eased to the door.

Trav worked the drawer out noiselessly. He leafed through a scattering of uninteresting papers and assorted articles. He closed that drawer and pulled out the next. It came out with a protesting squeak. He saw papers and odds and ends, none proving to be of interest. The third drawer revealed an oily .38 revolver with stubby nose and beneath it a small tied bundle of papers. These he took out and turned over in his hands. On the bottom side was a newspaper clipping and he did not have to read the story. The accusing headline on the faded paper had long since branded itself into his brain. He read:

TRAVIS PARKER KICKED OUT OF TEXAS RANGERS.

Just as he was about to explore further into the packet, Rotan cleared his throat at the doorway.

Hurriedly, Trav replaced the papers, then the gun, and shoved at the drawer. It twisted crazily and stuck. He seesawed it until it gave, hating the accusing squeak it made on the rough wood slides.

Rotan said heartily, 'Howdy-do, lady.'

Trav barely got from behind the desk before Rotan stepped back and fought off his hat. And as Rotan gave ground, a woman brushed past him, entering the room with a silky swish of loose skirt folds.

She was a young woman, robustly proportioned, wearing gem-set earrings, a Spanish comb in her hair, and a painted on smile. She turned alert eyes on Rotan for a quick study, then more hopefully across the room to Trav who tried to inch farther from the judge's desk.

Her red mouth came to a small pucker of indecision. She moved assuredly and as she came into the room her low-necklined dress played back the sheening lamp colors from her full, accented bosom. Trav saw that her features were powdered not quite enough to hide the little weather lines, but she carried herself youthfully. Not much older, if any, than he was. The kind of woman, he thought, who would playfully clutch a man's coat, push a sprig of early bluebonnets into the lapel and give him a gleaming remember last-night look before he went out to see what the Tonkawa invaders wanted. Perfect running mate, he figured, for a man who claimed to own the country and everybody in it.

He hoped she had not heard the drawer sliding. He said. 'You're Mrs. Denver Smith, I guess. We were invited—'

'You must be Mr. Parker.' She came around the desk. The full upturned face stopped only inches away. He felt a firm hand slide into his.

'I am. That's Rotan over there.'

'My husband told me—what you did this afternoon.' Her hand stayed longer than he knew what to do with it. Also all that white flesh kept glistening far down where the throat of her dress vented deep between the rounded swell of her breasts. He became painfully conscious of his long accumulation of trail dirt and saddle smell. His glance swung around and caught the whiskey bottle.

'Join us?'

'No, thank you. But you two go right ahead.'

'All right. We will.'

Rotan plodded over. 'Now you're talkin' sense. Nice place you got here, Mrs. Smith.'

'I like to see a man enjoy good whiskey.' She

63

laughed easily. 'The judge said you earned it. Also, there's a room for you upstairs.'

Trav took the jolt of the drink. 'We appreciate your hospitality, Mrs. Smith.'

'Everyone calls me Wilda.'

That was jumping the plover a little fast for his gun, he thought. But Brazos Pass was an unpredictable place, and the people in it, from the time he'd been shot trying to burglarize the judge's store for beans and flour, to now, when the judge's sturdy young wife was saying call her by her first name.

She spoke seriously. 'Do you think the Indians will stay peaceful tonight? Everyone is holding rifles at their windows. Such a bother!'

'There'll be no trouble tonight. Is the judge back yet?'

'He'll be here soon, I imagine. You're to go up to your room, if you care to. Would you like to take the bottle with you?'

Rotan said, 'Yes ma'am!'

At the doorway, as they moved out, she touched Trav's arm. 'I want to thank you again for getting my husband out of a bad fix. He can be so very—obstinate.'

'There's one thing—Wilda.'

'Yes?'

'A man who works for your husband, named Cabbo. He killed a man over at Karnack's house. Gus Jenkins. I was—'

Before he could finish, she gasped and clutched the door facing for support. The red

64

painted smile changed to open-mouthed shock. She breathed, 'Gus Jenkins?'

'Yes. Jenkins has a daughter somewhere in the settlement. I was wondering if you or some other woman would be kind enough to see if there's anything can be done for her tonight? It's a bad blow, a mighty bad thing.'

The frank eyes had clouded and her powdered cheeks looked whiter. She worked her mouth twice before words came. 'I—I'll go to see her. She's at the Rigsby house.'

'Will she stand up under the trouble all right, you think?'

He could see that she was badly shaken. Her words were barely audible. 'Mary's a very strong girl. It's a cruel thing for her. But we are used to cruel things happening out here.'

'This was plain coyote. Cabbo shot Jenkins in the back.'

He saw the little shudder go over her. 'A very cruel thing,' she murmured again. 'I had no idea—' Her words choked off.

'I'd like for Mary to be told I'll be glad to do anything I can, to help—'

'I'll see that she's told that, Mr. Parker.'

Because he felt sympathy for her, or wanted to be gentle, or just for friendliness to repay her own, he said, 'My friends call me Trav.'

Upstairs, in the bedroom, he peeled off his dirty clothes and set about examining the leg wound. Rotan poured from the bottle and said to nobody: 'My friends call me Rotan, too. But

65

usually not the first ten or fifteen seconds.'

Trav grunted. He propped a chair under the doorknob. 'Open the saddle roll and find the old razor. You know, I don't like this place. Not the way it looks, not the way it smells, not anybody in it.'

'I got the same feeling in my gizzard. What's the game here?'

'Judge Denver Smith owns a newspaper clipping and he's kept it a long time. It was in that drawer.'

'About you?'

'This one had the headline: Travis Parker Kicked Out of Texas Rangers.'

'Uh-oh.'

Trav put the big bowl on the floor, poured water from the white crockery pitcher, dropped in a bar of soap, and began to bathe the wound. Maybe the whiskey exaggerated the way he felt, but not very much. Sometimes everything felt wrong about a place or a situation, and he had learned to trust his own instincts. He stopped and reached for his gunbelt. He pulled the .45 and placed it on the floor beside the wash bowl six inches from his hand.

Rotan said, 'It's like that, huh?'

'In those days we had hunches. If a man paid attention to 'em he was likely to live longer. My father told me that. Every old Ranger said so.'

Rotan opened the saddle roll and loosened

his prized stolen blanket to dig for the razor. He kept his gun on when he shaved.

The new clothes fitted well enough. The water and soap and razor could make a tramp rider feel like a new man. The wound looked all right, too, in spite of the little blood drops speckling the edges of the crusty scab. Trav tied it up anew with torn strips from a towel. Taking his turn at the hand-size cracked mirror, he worked the razor and tried to separate the thoughts which were strung across his mind like a row of blackbirds fluttering on a fence.

Nowhere, in all the past, as far as he could remember, had his search turned up the name of Denver Smith. Not unless some things had dropped from his memory during the half-alive time in the Tonkawa camp. He had backtracked his troubles to Abilene, hunting like a bloodhound for just any small scent to start on, but his patient probings had never raised such a name. Jack Hinton, yes. That was the man who had contracted to move the Bradshaw herd from Texas to Kansas. And the name of Gus Jenkins had come into it, somewhere, as having been one of Hinton's riders. But the names of the other men who had left Abilene with Hinton had remained unknown.

What had Jenkins said, back in the nester house? Oh, yes. *If I told you that I'd get killed.*

Who would have killed him? Well, they had

been talking about Jack Hinton. He had been prodding Jenkins for information on Hinton, hadn't he? Trav paused with the razor. Jenkins hadn't said that Jack Hinton would kill him. Not by name. But wasn't it the same thing?

He frowned, studying his own face. The blurred mirror, peeled out in spots, seemed to fleck with movement in its stained crack lines. The lamp light put weak yellow on the dark window behind his back and the window relayed the gleams in flickering shadow play into the speckled mirror. Beyond the reflection of his head he could see a part of Rotan's stretched-out booted legs on the bed.

So somebody had sent Eckhart to ambush Jenkins, and they had done it not long after he and Rotan entered the country, making inquiries here and there. And then somebody had sent Cabbo to team up with Eckhart on the job, evidently to make sure there was no slip-up. And whatever was in it for the killer, it had been enough to make Cabbo go wild and shoot Jenkins in front of five or six men. And Cabbo's initial challenge, seemingly so senseless when they had first entered Kamack's, now seemed to have purpose behind it. Cabbo had meant to start trouble and that insulting reference to Mary Jenkins had been his move to pull her father into gun play. And that was how Cabbo meant to do his job. He'd had Jenkins identified by then and he'd meant to kill him and he hadn't cared

68

how many witnesses saw him do it.

And Cabbo worked for judge Denver Smith.

Trav speculated that sixty thousand dollars stolen two years ago off a near-dead rider in the Territory would be about right to start a secret Comanche trade enterprise up here where Texas law was too far off to interfere, or even know. Judge Denver Smith came into sharper focus, then, as he tried to piece it together.

The man's crazy vanity and love of his own grandeur were reflected in his challenging belligerence and big red horse and fool showoff with the Indians. It showed in this isolated saloon, where the judge played a lordly role, big and fancy, even with no customers but his own gun crews. The wife he had brought along displayed it, too. Sixty thousand dollars worth of playing king up at the top of Texas, and a shapely abundance of healthy queen to keep him company in both his public and private domains.

Rotan flopped his foot. Trav caught its movement in the mirror.

'You thinking what I am, Rotan?'

'Sure. It's him.'

'Chances are.'

'You Rangers knew how to get at a thing. I'm lettin' you sack this one up.'

The boot toe moved again in the mirror. Only it was not the boot. Just reflections of the light. Trav caught up cupped palms of water and rubbed off the last of the lather. He had to see Mary Jenkins. Tonight if possible.

'Rotan. Don't move any part of your body, don't turn your head or anything. Just move your foot a little.'

He watched the mirror. Rotan said, 'I moved it.'

The sixgun lay beside the basin on the wash stand. Trav ran a comb through his hair, leaning close to the mirror as if to nicely set the part. His right hand came down in front of his body. He closed his fingers over the butt of the Colt.

His fist wrapped up the solid weight of the gun as he whirled, ducking his shoulders, and he came about crouching, with the gun spitting a red-streaked blast of fire at the window. He didn't want to kill. He sent the shot high.

Glass tinkled to the floor. A faint clatter sounded outside and Trav hurried to the window. Keeping to the side of it he looked out to the blackness of the night. When his vision fitted itself to the darkness he caught fleeting sight of a dark form hurdling down the outside stairway from the second-floor gallery. Before he could raise the window, the man vanished around the back corner of the 'dobe wall.

Rotan crowded up, his Peacemaker in hand.

'What—the hell? We have a spy out there?'

'He was watching us from the porch, with just a hat showing at the edge of the window. I couldn't see what he looked like.'

'You hit him?'

'Don't think so. Didn't try to.'

Rotan fixed Trav with squinted eyes. 'Spooky damn place.'

They talked in undertones for a few minutes. Then, as Trav expected, a knocking came at the door. He removed the chair and jerked the door inward.

Wilda Smith caught at her throat in a startled movement. If he had ever seen stark fear deep in a woman's soul, he was seeing it now in her pleading eyes. But she fought to control the expression. 'The shot?' Imploringly, she touched his arm. 'I was afraid—'

He relaxed and holstered the gun. He chuckled easily. 'The darn thing went off. Afraid I owe you for a window glass. That whiskey of your husband's made me a little careless,'

'Oh. I'm glad that's all it was.'

'What did you think it might be?'

She did not reply to that. She stood in the doorway for an awkward moment, looking at the broken window. 'The judge is downstairs,' she said. 'He wants you to help him plan a talk with the Tonkawa chief.'

'Did you see Mary?'

Her voice went strangely harsh. 'I went to Rigsby's, yes. She asked that you see her tonight.'

Her composure seemed to return. She looked at Trav now with a new expression. 'Clothes and a shave make a difference in a man.'

He just nodded. She could take up the rope slack or leave it. He waited. She took it up.

'Would you—please step out here just a minute—Trav?'

In the hallway, with the door pulled closed against Rotan's tight-squinted disfavor, Wilda touched his arm again. Even in this dim light, worry showed beneath the surface of her tilted face. She kept her voice low. 'I have to tell you something. You're not fooling me about that shot. You should leave here. At once!'

'First, why do you say you have to tell me?'

Her chin went down. Her index finger twisted nervously into the sleeve of his new shirt. He could barely hear her murmur. 'I haven't seen any man—any new man—of my age-in a long time. You can't know what it's been like here, all these months.'

'You're married,' Trav said. 'You're not supposed to see any other man, any kind, any time.'

'I'm a woman!' she whispered fiercely. 'This is a lonely land!'

She was a woman, all right. A woman of bountiful promise and unbridled willingness. If he had heard her right, she was offering this risk to bring him a warning in exchange for . . . what?

72

He said, 'I wonder if I understand you.'

'I'm clutching at any straw. I want you to take me away from here.'

'You think I ought to get out, and you want to get out with me? Is that what you're proposing?'

'I'm afraid! I ask your help. Yes, that's what I mean.'

'Well, excuse me for not understanding everything. But you seem to have plenty of money. Why don't you just leave?'

'I'm like a—a prisoner here. There's no way to get out. Please! Will you take me?'

'How do you mean that?'

She increased her grip on his arm. 'Any way you want me to mean it.'

'You're frank enough.'

She raised her face to stare up at him and her bold eyes did not waver. 'I'd have no shame with you, just so you'll help me get away. I'm going crazy in this place!' Her voice caught. 'You can't know what this lonely country has been like!'

'Does the judge know how you feel?'

'He would kill me or anyone who crossed him. That's why I had to warn you.'

'Are you honestly trying to help me? Why this warning? You want to tell me more about that?'

She threw a frightened look over her shoulder toward the head of the stairs. 'Not here. Later. Tonight. He's down in the office

73

now. His men—he has spies, everywhere. Raffer—'

'Where will we meet?'

'I'll let you know.' She pushed back from him, raising her hand to brush a wisp of hair back from her forehead. Her features regained composure. 'We'll have to be careful.'

'Tell me one thing now,' he whispered. There might not be any *later* and he had to push his opportunity fast. She was willing to make a trade. Whatever else might be stirring her deep inner feminine being, she had come to give him warning. 'You can tell me this—now! Later, maybe we'll make a trade. But I want this!'

'Yes?'

'Your husband—is his name really Denver Smith?'

Wilda leaned back to search his face in the faint light. Her tone was puzzled. 'Of course. Why do you ask?'

He caught her firm upper arm in a tight grip. He pulled her so close to him that the fabric of her dress brushed its softness across him.

'Let's start with the truth. I want to know this—is your husband Jack Hinton?'

For a moment she did not move. The yielding fullness of her bosom stayed pressed against him. Then she pulled back abruptly.

'Jack Hinton? Of course not!' she said hotly. 'I'm not lying to you, Trav. I thought you

74

knew.'

He felt a stab of disappointment. 'Thought I knew what?'

'Please, I'm afraid for us to talk longer here.' Again she glanced back worriedly toward the stairs. 'I'll get word to you where we can meet tonight.'

'Tell me!' he gritted. 'What was it you thought I knew? You both have me figured. You know who Travis Parker is.

'Yes, he knows.'

'What does it mean to him?'

'He's—uncertain. Afraid.'

'Well, what was it you thought I knew about Jack Hinton?'

She raised her troubled face pleadingly to his again, and if he had ever seen complete honesty in a woman's eyes, he saw it now.

'Gus Jenkins,' she said. 'I thought you knew Gus Jenkins was Jack Hinton.'

Then she gave his arm a parting squeeze, and fled.

CHAPTER SIX

Rotan said, 'What's the matter, boy?'

'I've just been pole-axed.'

'What'd she do?'

'Jenkins wasn't all we lost. We lost Jack Hinton at the same time. Jenkins—he was

Hinton.'

'What? Say that again!'

Trav told him about Wilda's disclosure.

'Somewhere, we got the wrong rumor, the garbled information,' Trav went on. 'I've always been afraid it could happen that way. I picked up Jenkins' name somewhere, maybe tenth-hand in that Abilene saloon. Maybe he used two names, maybe he picked Jenkins before the trouble, or after. We don't know the reason. All the threads we had to go on were thin ones in the first place. And all the trails were old and cold.'

They each thought back, re-working the many little siftings and clues and rumors. It had been a needle-in-a-haystack hunt and a mighty big haystack to hunt in. As Trav reconstructed it, talking with Rotan now, he had come back to consciousness after unknown weeks of crude treatment in the Tonkawa camp in the Territory with the fixed belief that Jack Hinton had been his ambusher. Months later, when he left the Tonks and started his search, he had somewhere picked up the name of Gus Jenkins as one who had ridden out of Abilene with Hinton. His information could have been mixed up. So the fruitless hunt for a trace of Hinton had then turned into a trailing of Jenkins with no ghost of suspicion that they might be the same man.

Rotan thought it all over. 'Hinton or no

Hinton, Gus Jenkins wasn't what I figured a bad man.'

'The girl kept trying to say he had no part in that robbery.'

'You be mighty careful,' Rotan warned. 'You can't tell who's who in this damned country.'

But Trav thought he was in no immediate danger and said so. 'The judge needs somebody to dicker with Blue Knife and I'm his best bet for that. It's a high card we hold for the time being, anyhow. You stand by till I get a better tally on Denver Smith and a chance to see Mary. I'm worried about what might happen to her. There might be some more Eckharts and Cabbos around.',

Trav eased through the door and descended the stairway. When he entered the office, he found the judge standing behind the desk lighting a slim cigar.

'What the hell was that shot up there?' the judge demanded.

'Rotan got careless. His gun went off.'

'Careless is right. You have a talk with my wife up there?'

The question could be a trap, either way. How much did the man know about his wife? 'Yes, we met Mrs. Smith. Thanks for the new clothes and whiskey. You folks have been right hospitable, judge.'

'Wilda is a right hospitable woman.'

Trav ignored whatever implication Smith might have intended and cut across all pretense. 'Cliff Cabbo worked for you, you said. Why did he kill Jenkins? Was that part of his working for you?'

The judge affected a careless gesture. 'Damned nester.'

'That's not what I asked you.'

The judge studied him through the cigar smoke and changed his tone.

'Now let's take up one thing at a time, Parker.' The big man made a pretense of a smile and friendly heartiness. 'This whole settlement is practically in a state of siege, you might say, and we got to do something about it. You can be useful to me. I can pay a price. I like the way you handled those Tonks out there today.'

'You didn't make it any easier. Anybody ever tell you, Smith, that even a bull knows better than to throw his weight at quicksand?'

The fictitious friendliness drained off. The judge worked a glance down to the bottom desk drawer. The newspaper headline down there flashed across Trav's mind. The judge murmured, 'One thing I've wondered about you, Parker. Whether you showed up here just on your own——or maybe in some official capacity.'

With the loaded words aimed right at him, Trav caught a glimmer of what might be bothering the judge the most. Even more than the Tonkawas. He would not know, and he might be worried, about Trav's present status with the Rangers. For all he could guess at the moment, the judge might be gnawed by the possibility that Trav and Rotan were the forerunners of a full move—in on this Cap Rock empire by a whole company coming to open up this forgotten land. No man, not even one as big as the judge, could rest easy over seeds of speculation if he had something to hide.

'Like you said,' Trav told him, 'let's take up one thing at a time.'

The judge masked whatever had rankled him and put on the friendliness again.

'I could use you, Parker. I'm prepared to make it worth while. I like what I got up here and I wouldn't like to see it disturbed. Now about those Indians. The whole settlement's on edge tonight. The nester families are crowding all the houses and everybody's at their windows with rifles. I want to get those bastard Tonks off my back and out of here.'

Trav decided then that he would play out the cards with the man. If the judge was fighting for time, so was he, and to no less a degree of desperation.

'We might start our trade, judge, with the understanding that nobody comes spying at my window.'

The judge started to reply, and then Trav heard the footsteps behind him.

'Come in, Raffer,' the judge said.

Trav turned toward the door. He saw a fox-faced man of about thirty with a white scar under one ear, blond brows crowded together, and an absolutely blank expression on his sun-peeled face. Raffer's mouth hung slightly open and wet. His long, slack arms ended in claw-sharp fingers that tickled the fringe of his double gun holsters, and on the tight black shirt that showed all his muscles he sported a silver-plated star.

That and one more thing. A brown scorched streak showed across the side of his flat-topped white hat.

'Raffer's my law here,' judge Smith said. 'This is Travis Parker, Raffer. We're discussing how to handle those Tonkawas.'

Raffer stared at Trav without expression or acknowledgment, and Trav thought of all the hired killers he had known down the dim past. He let his own roving, up-and-down stare come to rest on the streak across Raffer's hat.

'That's an unusual decoration you got on your headgear, Raffer. Somebody came close with that one.'

And it happened not over an hour ago, he told himself. Right outside that window.

Raffer spoke for the first time, blankly and to the judge. 'Does Parker suffer from too much curiosity?'

'No—from not enough!' Trav snapped. 'All right, judge. You want me to deal with the Tonks. What do I get? This has all been one-sided up to now.'

The judge leaned back. Raffer glided slowly to a corner and remained on his feet, his fingernails still scratching the twin holsters. The judge murmured, 'You'd be surprised how one-sided it can be.'

The bartender came to the doorway. He wore a sixgun now, his apron was off and two slack-shouldered men with rifles sauntered in behind him.

'Pete and Brister,' the bartender growled. 'They want to know if this bird is going to the Tonk camp and if you still want them to chaperone him.'

The pair with the rifles watched Trav. Judge Smith stood up.

'They'll ride along with you, Parker. It's just for your protection. We wouldn't want anything to happen to you. Pete and Brister know Indians pretty well.'

'Thanks. But I don't need chaperones. This pair least of all.' He knew the judge meant for them to be his captors, not his bodyguard, and he also concluded that his first move, once he was out of there, had better be a talk with Mary Jenkins. He saw the judge deliberate a moment, then gesture indifference.

'All right, do it your own way. Get out there now and see what you can do with Blue Knife.'

'What are you willing to pay him to pull out?'

'Make the best trade you can. Steers, cloth, tobacco, trade stuff. The store's full of junk I could give them.'

'Judge, you may not figure these Tonks just right. Remember they've been chewed up by the Comanches for years. And they know where the Comanches come for guns and whiskey. It's not just a bolt of calico they're after. They want some guns and whiskey, too—and maybe they want even worse to ride in their last fight against white men by charging down on this settlement and cutting some scalps.'

'No guns!' the judge said with finality.

'They're reserved for the Comanches? Is that it, judge?'

Judge Denver Smith almost seemed to be enjoying this. 'What makes you think so?' he asked genially.

Trav circled his hand. 'All this layout. Hired gunmen at your coattails. Big fine saloon with nobody in a hundred miles to be customers. Big store but not enough people here to crowd a prairie dog hole. You got a great place. A big front. Something has to pay for it.'

Brister, Pete, and Raffer the lawman held their attention on the judge as if awaiting a signal.

But the judge kept his composure. 'Parker, I get all the answers I want here, and I don't have to give any. You're in no position to ask questions. We might as well get that straight.'

'Yeah. I remember. You were going to handle all the answers out there with the

Tonks. You want to tell me about Cabbo now? What did you offer him and Eckhart to shut up Jenkins for good?'

A tightening of Smith's jaw showed his anger had only been smoldering. 'You must have hit that whiskey a little fast. I'm giving you a lot of rope, Parker. A man doesn't usually make that much gab to me and retain his health.'

In the long silence that followed, Trav realized that he had pushed the judge as far as would be safe. He had to find Mary Jenkins before these fine cutthroats in the room were goaded to violence.

'I'll go for the Tonkawa camp now,' he said.

'You come back and tell me,' the judge said. 'Raffer, you others, stay here a minute.'

Trav made the long walk through the empty saloon, angled down the dark deserted street, and roused the youth at the stables. He got his horse, saddled, and asked the boy: 'Where's the Rigsby house?'

'Last house north.'

At Rigsby's he dismounted and knocked on the door. Somebody opened it a crack and demanded, 'All right, what'd you want?'

'This Rigsby's house?'

'Yeah. Say, this is Parker, ain't it?'

The door opened and revealed Trav in the thin starlight. The other man said, 'I'm Drain. We rode in together.'

'I'm looking for Mary Jenkins, Drain.'

'Mary?' Drain repeated in a surprised tone.

'Yes. I heard she was here.'

Another man joined Drain in the doorway. Drain turned to him. 'Fellow Parker, looking for Mary. What'd you make of that, Rigsby?'

'Haven't you been at the Brazos Palace?' Rigsby asked.

'That's right.'

Rigsby shook his head and turned to Drain. 'I thought she'd gone to see him.'

Drain said, 'She's been gone an hour, Parker. A man came to get her. He said you wanted to see her at the judge's place. You mean she hasn't been there?'

Trav felt the rat-like play of weakness slither through his knees. 'Who was the man who came after her?'

'Why it was Raffer,' Rigsby said. 'The judge's law man.'

'They leave walking?'

'No, he had an extra horse for her.'

Mrs. Drain crowded out between the two men. 'Is anything wrong?'

'Listen, you folks,' Trav said slowly. It was too much to hope, but he would try it. 'Are any of you willing to tell me about the judge, and about Gus Jenkins, and about this whole settlement of Brazos Pass? Any of you willing to say why Cabbo shot Jenkins? You people from the little spreads around here—has the judge and his crew got their feet on your necks? Who'll talk to me about these things?'

Nothing but dead silence answered him. Then Drain's mouth came close to his ear. 'Couple of the judge's men in the house with us,' he whispered. 'You better get along.' He added pleadingly, 'For God's sake, *find* Mary!'

More loudly, he said, 'Well, now, we don't like prying people around here. We got enough to worry about as it is, watching for the Indians to attack.'

Rigsby agreed. 'If you want to do something, mister, you can take your turn on guard tonight like the rest of us have got to do.'

Trav backed away from the door, down the steps, and mounted. Then he reined the buckskin and drove in the spurs. He struck south for the open prairie and Blue Knife's camp.

CHAPTER SEVEN

Bee-lah.

A pretty name, Bee-lah. Soft eyes to match it. Brown, firm in the thighs, surging with her springtime; a ferociousness in her love that only Indians had. The prettiest Tonkawa woman he had ever seen. And his, once, same as deeded land. Well, somewhere in the Territory, Bee-lah was a buck's property by now, probably Fox One-Eye's, and a bargain at

85

twenty ponies, as the Tonkawas priced their women.

Funny thing. Months on end he'd starved for a woman, and tonight he had three too many closing him. Two in the present and one in the past. The Tonkawas never forgot anything. Especially anything like Blue Knife's ceremonious gift of Bee-lah to the white man, which was like parting with a prize string of war ponies.

So he had to ride straight into the dark angry midst of them, on a night blacker than all the spades in the deck. He'd never see a blade until he felt it, if that was the way some young Tonk wanted to add coup.

Each dark bush clump and hooting owl became a menace. His nervousness, either by smell or rein touch, transmitted itself to the mustang. The ride into the edgy Tonkawas' camp was nothing for a white man to relish in daytime, let alone at night. Neither was the decision. Stay or run?

The horse showed its tiredness and behaved meanly, until man and mustang traded their fear-smelly sweat odors and contested one another on every unhappy stride into the blackness. The horse knew better than the man that night was no time to take up again the hurting process of going somewhere. The animal kept throwing its head back, shying like its rider at each ghostly spread-arm bush that stood like a blind dwarf. For a time the mustang tried to circle cunningly to the back trail, ambling off sideways with neck curved as if to avoid something ahead. Trav matched his wits against this and for the third time caught himself fingering the butt of his gun just to prove it was still there. Then he worked the handle of his sheathed knife under his jacket closer to reach.

A play of wind brought the faint smell of greasy smoke. The Indian camp was not far off.

A dust devil spun up immediately ahead. It whirled off on its slithering business to nowhere in the blackness. Both man and mustang jerked nervously. The mustang stopped. It was asking the man if he wanted to go farther.

Far back, Trav heard the other horses. Unmistakable hoof sounds, somewhere behind him. The mustang heard and flung its head. An owl hoot came trembling out of the void.

Trav started up, stopped again, listened. The other sounds stopped, too. Or else it had all been imagination.

He walked the mustang ahead. The logic of escape beat against his brain, and then he solved the problem by chucking reason out altogether. He kept riding.

The smoke smell whipped in again, and he knew the grove lay close ahead. Tobacco, padded with singed sumac, underlaid with grease odors from earlier cook fires. A

87

pungent, telltale odor. Nothing else like it.

Now a bush moved differently. He loosened the sixgun. The bush separated into two dark forms. One of these stepped forward. He could see by imagination the chilled brown tattooed body with its buckskin shoulder piece and the lone crow-tail feather poking up beside the buck's ear. He pulled up.

'Death-In-The-Ribs comes back to his friends in peace.'

The lookout said, 'Blue Knife has waited.'

The shadowy form merged again with the bulk of a fat cedar. Alongside this, Trav murmured in Tonkawa, 'I would like to know if I have been followed.'

'The night is not marching alone.'

'You heard them, too?'

An indistinguishable grunt. The Indian went invisible. Nothing remained but the wind stroking the cedar. Blue Knife's band was on edge, else there would have been no outguards. He knew how the Tonkawas disliked the darkness. Trav heeled the mustang into motion.

As he advanced into the first trees, red coals began to show to him like wildcat eyes where the fires had been banked. Around these, blanketed forms made dark blobs on the grass. Other Indians stood, tall shapes with rifles ready. One came forward.

'This is Fire Feather.'

'A brave warrior. My friend.'

Another towered beside Fire Feather. 'White man walk now. This is Fox One-Eye.'

Trav could think of no proper response to Fox as he dismounted. Fox had hopefully stolen and saved ponies for a year, to the amusement of the whole village, to meet Blue Knife's price on Bee-lah, a choice property. Then the chief had abruptly made her his gift to the dead white man who lived. The squaws had laughed openly at the chagrined Fox. Trav could only wish now that Fox One-Eye had stayed in the Territory.

Without further talk they headed him toward the pointed shadow of a *tipi*. Another Indian glided alongside and roughly caught his arm. Trav submitted, and they brought him to the tall cone of hide and pulled back the calfskin covering. Stooping, he saw Blue Knife inside, faintly outlined by the glow of a small fire. The chief, an unmoving lump of deerskin trappings and feathers, muttered, 'Death-In-The-Ribs,' without turning. The buck released his arm. Fox tapped him sharply upon the shoulder with a rifle barrel. Trav took a final gulp of the night air and crawled inside.

On the spur of the moment he extended his hand. He thought it would hang in the air eternally before Blue Knife came alive and grudgingly responded to the white man's style of greeting.

'Where are supplies the village promised?'

'They will come. I'm here to see what my

brothers need. I will send the first wagon at daybreak.'

Blue Knife gazed steadily into the nibbling flames. When he spoke again, it was from far back in the caves of his memory. 'Young white man run away. He left the chief's daughter that had been Blue Knife's gift to him. A gift refused. For the Tonkawas, that was insult.'

'I thought it better for her to stay with her people. I meant no insult.'

'Bee-lah worth twenty ponies. After that, no more than fifteen.'

'She was still worth twenty.' He hoped Blue Knife would know what he meant by that.

But it backfired. Blue Knife shook his head. 'That was more insult.'

'A white man calls it a matter of honor.'

'Indian not understand,' Blue Knife said testily. 'White man take all Tehanna land,' motioning to the whole of Texas. 'But you not take wedding night with Bee-lah.'

'She told you?'

'No. Fox find out. He cheat me out of five ponies, then tell me and laugh.'

Discussing Bee-lah like a chattel made Trav uncomfortable. Blue Knife added craftily, 'You come back, live with us, buy Bee-lah from Fox. All our people be happy you come again. Need white friend's wisdom.'

The Tonk was going to be touchy about the past. The old man had a memory as lasting as rawhide. Blue Knife liked to pull out an old

90

hurt and fondle it again like something shiny picked off the ground just a while ago.

'The Tonkawas starve,' Blue Knife grumbled. 'White men's handshakes, white men's lies. My people are dying.'

'I have come tonight to help the Tonkawas.'

'There is bad medicine in the settlement. My warriors ask, is Death-In-The-Ribs one of them? Why you here?'

'I am not one of them in the village. Tell your warriors that. The people there are my enemies. I need the help of Blue Knife.'

He heard a scuffle at the opening. Several painted shapes pushed through. The tall and muscular warriors crowded in and settled down behind the chief. Trav scanned their features, remembering some of them, and wished again that Fox One-Eye was not one of the chiefs council.

Blue Knife, as if moved to a performance before his council, made a sudden impassioned gesture with a tattooed arm and loosed a fury of Tonkawa words upon the white settlement of Brazos Pass, ending it with a foul noun spat out in English.

A strained silence blanketed everything after Blue Knife's tirade. Fox One-Eye seemed to be piercing Trav with both his blackened blank socket and the flames reflected in his good orb. The closeness of the hide *tipi* made the inside animal hot and smelly.

Blue Knife decided it was time to

acknowledge an old friendship. His arm moved. With relief, Trav accepted the pipe.

Nobody spoke until the longnecked pipe had made its rounds. Trav waited, watching the fire, refraining from directly looking at the others. They watched the fire, too, and then Blue Knife began the expected recital.

He started at the beginning and verbally fingered off his string of woes in a bitter account of the tribulations of his people.

As it had been in those interminable nights of Trav's patient listening in the Territory, the chiefs lament was for the old times of his fathers. Those glories, he said, had gone down like a hurt bird with spent wings in a sleet storm. Once the Tonkawas had built their *wetsoxan* lodges of willow sticks and cane in the warmth of the Neches timbers. There they had tilled their corn patches and stayed together. Fat *cibolo* were to be found in the wallows to the west. As a young chief, Blue Knife and his hunters always came in with meat in plenty. The tribe celebrated the big hunts with their Wolf Dance, and their troubles had been few, except when the hated Comanches came raiding out of the distant plains. Each man had his lodge, and as many squaws as he had ponies or hides to trade for them. And their natural hospitality extended to the first white man who came, serving them as guides and even lending them wives or maidens on their overnight visits. The

Tonkawas had expected to live in peace with their new white neighbors.

Then the white men changed. Handshakes concealed snakes of treachery, and what had been offered the whites as friends they began to take by force. All this Travis Parker had heard before from the same shriveled and ugly creature who mouthed it now with rising viciousness.

Once Blue Knife stopped suddenly and made an accusing sign: was the white man across the fire listening? just as impatiently, Trav flashed his hand in the sign for Blue Knife to continue. He knew the thing to do was to maintain patience. His own troubles had to be held suspended. The dangers that might now be confronting Mary Jenkins, the problem, with Denver Smith, the possibility of getting needed information from Wilda, the safety of Rotan . . . His own disheveled world had to stop in its turning while this wronged and vindictive chief-with-his-glory-gone recounted woes.

Now, Blue Knife went on, the Tonkawas languished in their hated Territory retreat, hazed by the Comanches on the one hand and starved on the other by white man's abandonment. They had come by enough arms, finally, for this expedition of revenge. Then Trav's ears pricked up when Blue Knife said: 'We die in the stink of our hunger or we die in the better way, the Indian way, in battle against our enemies. We have ridden on this long journey to make our decision.'

In the pause, Trav asked if the decision had been made. Blue Knife hesitated. The bucks behind him tensed. Blue Knife's reply was involved and labored. He said that desperation had sent him and his best warriors, with what rifles they had, on this journey which they knew might be their last. Their decision depended upon what they found here at the mysterious headwaters of the Brazos.

Trav began to get in his questions. Did the Tonkawas know for certain that the chief of the white settlement supplied the Comanches? What was the procedure?

They had long known, Blue Knife replied. The Comanches stole cattle and horses, in Mexico and everywhere, for the white chief of Brazos Pass, receiving guns, ammunition and whiskey in return. Sarcastically Blue Knife asked, where did the white fathers *think* the Comanches and Kiowas got their guns and bullets for all the massacres up and down the length of Texas? Did they suppose the Comanches made them with their own hands out of boughs that grew on black walnut trees?

Where did the dealings take place, Trav wanted to know.

At Denver Smith's ranch headquarters. Blue Knife pointed at the west wall of the hide tent. Tonkawa scouts had seen the place, a rock house built like a fort. They had stalked

94

Comanche-guided herd outfits to the source, had seen with their own eyes the Comanches returning with pack ponies heavily loaded. Trav pressed for the location of the rock house. A buck answered for Blue Knife, and Trav worked it out of him, until he thought he knew the direction and distance. He felt the blood pound up in his ears, for here was new hope. That place might yield some clue to Denver Smith's past. He resolved that he would search Smith's ranch house—if he could get out of Brazos Pass long enough to do it.

And now, what of the night of the ambush? Could they pull out the feathers of its details again for him?

The Indian named Tamak talked with his hands and a word mixture of Tonkawa and Texas phrases. Tamak said he and other Tonkawa scouts had known for two or three days that one man was riding southward and that three men were following him.

Fire Feather cut in to relate that the three whites had engaged in big angry talk. In their own camp, at sundown of that night. Did the Indians hear a name spoken? Fire Feather considered. Trav saw that he was about to speak. But then Fire Feather locked his jaws.

He knew a name, Trav guessed quickly. This Indian knew it, but he did not know how to say it except in his ears. It was a heard sound, not a mouth one, to Fire Feather.

'Did it sound like this?' Trav asked slowly.

'Jenkins. Jenkins.'

Fire Feather thought hard.

'No. Up here,' touching his head, 'Fire Feather not hear that word.'

'Hinton? Jack Hinton?'

'No.'

'Listen long, brother. Are you sure?'

Fire Feather only looked baffled.

'Smith, then. *Sme-eth.* Does your head hear a sound like *Den-ver Smith*?'

Quickly, Tamak grunted an affirmative before Fire Feather could answer.

'Den-ver.'

'You were not as close to the camp as I was,' Fire Feather said heatedly.

'Word is like a mosquito gone,' Tamak complained.

'Den-ver,' Trav tried again. 'In their argument in camp, did one of them say that?'

Tamak nodded agreeably.

'Said what?'

'Hin-ton.'

'Oh, my God—I asked you that before! Is the mosquito word like Hin-ton, or does it buzz in your head like Denver?'

'Jack!' Fire Feather spoke and folded his arms as if he had settled it.

'What?'

'Men mad. Loud word, *Jack!*'

'You heard that word, Fire Feather?'

'Loud. Like a kick dog.'

'Say it again.'

'Jack.'

'What do you say to that, Tamak?'

'Jacinton.' He sounded it like *Walk-in-ton*.

'Jack Hinton?'

'I was closer than Tamak,' Fire Feather growled.

Trav knuckled his chin. 'What Death-In-The-Ribs begs of his brothers is the name of a white man heard that night. Listen close to the mosquito singing in your head. Does its wings whisper now a sound like Jack Hinton?'

Fire Feather stared belligerently at Tamak, who looked at Fire Feather and then at the coals. Fox One-Eye elaborately folded his arms over his white streaked chest, an ostentatious movement as if he knew something far and above this confusion of lesser men. Trav caught this, but damned if he was going to ask Bee-lah's bargain-maker a direct question.

'It is the word I hear,' Fire Feather said. 'I was as close as a lobo will go to a sleeping dove on a low limb.'

'It is the word I hear,' Tamak agreed.

Trav believed them. It was the word he had heard in the Abilene saloon and in the dives of Sanantone. It was Jack Hinton all over the place, and Jack Hinton was dead. What did he have here but more confusing signs on a washed-out trail?

So the one called Jack Hinton, what did he do after the argument? They never knew one man from another, Fire Feather said. They were watching from distant cover. It was just a word remembered. Two white men went off through the blackness toward the sleeping stranger. After a time, big shooting.

The third man?

He rode away in the night, alone.

Where? What direction?

In the direction of the Red River. Toward *Tehanna*, Texas.

Could it have been Jack Hinton who rode away?

Fire Feather shrugged. His brother come-alive should know that all this had happened in darkness like the underside of a blackbird's wing.

So they had found Travis Parker. Sprawled like dead with his gun out in his hand, at first daybreak in the greasewood on the brink of a redstone arroyo. His lost blood clotting its own flow, his horse and rig gone, and the green dung flies beginning to collect where his flesh showed a black hole. Then Fire Feather had heard the frightening ghost of a spoken word and they all retreated, because a dead man should make no sounds, and his spirit must be speaking to them.

They had found the other man, not far off, dead beyond doubt, with his brains blown out. And then they had summoned Blue Knife and other warriors. Returning, they found that Death-In-The-Ribs somehow had stuffed his own bandana into the rib hole and the blood flow had stopped. The dead man looked at them with the eyes of a live man who sees.

Trav tried to put their account into understandable parcels of fact. One man had ridden away before the ambush, proceeding southward, and this after an argument. Then two had ridden to the ambush. One had shot and robbed him, and then had killed the other. One of the three had the name of Jack Hinton, if he could believe Tamak's and Fire Feather's memory.

And that, he thought dejectedly, was exactly where he had started this dismal day. On the trail of a nester who might have known Jack Hinton—and the nester himself had been Jack Hinton, now dead. And the mysterious Hinton had a daughter who, at this moment, might be in danger of a half-crazy warlord of the region named Denver Smith who traded with the Comanches from a fort-like place somewhere in the roughs to the west. That was about the sum of it. He knew an urgency to find Mary Hinton. Gravely, he thanked them and stood to go.

Blue Knife raised hard-squinted eyes. The wrinkles worked. 'You send supplies?'

'At daylight. Food for your warriors.' As he stooped for the opening, a guttural word sounded at the far side of the *tipi*.

'Den-ver.'

Trav whirled. Fox One-Eye, with arms high

99

folded, had his socket and his good eye fastened on Fire Feather.

'Say that again, brother.'

'Men mad. Talk loud. Fox hear *Den-ver!*'

Trav searched quickly to Fire Feather, to Tamak, and back to Fox.

Carefully, he said, 'The men talked loud in the night. Fox hear the word—*Den-ver*?'

Slowly, Fox One-Eye filled his tattooed chest with air and self-importance. 'Fox closer than all the others. *Denver*. He there.'

Trav pierced the paint-streaked mask and believed him. Denver and Jack Hinton. Both. The trail had neared its end. He wanted to say, *Thank you brother—and give my regards to Bee-lah!* Instead, he made a sign word of commendation to Fox.

Jack Hinton.' Fire Feather was having no correction from his one-eyed neighbor.

'Den-ver!' Fox One-Eye snarled back at him.

Blue Knife upheld them both. 'My ears speak to me now. Those are the names told to me at the time.'

Tamak nodded. 'Hear two mosquitoes. Den-ver. Hin-ton.

Fox agreed. He snapped out one finger, then a second.

Trav's doubts were gone. 'They are enough. There will be whiskey for Blue Knife and his council.'

'We have helped our friend?'

'You have!'

They had put both Jack Hinton and Denver Smith on the scene that night of his near death. All he needed now was tangible *white* proof. One thing stood out stark and clear. Denver Smith already knew that Trav Parker had to be killed all over again, just as soon as the Tonkawa threat was lifted.

Trav said, 'Death-In-The-Ribs will visit his brothers again. I ask that you stay here, hold this camp. Let the white settlement see your war strength. Blue Knife would do well to parade his men in force when the village wakes up.

Shrewdly, the chief nodded understanding. 'Where there is fear of losing scalps, there will be more wagons of supplies for the Tonkawas.'

With a quick look back, just to make sure Fox kept his place, Trav ducked from the *tipi* and hurried into the night. He had to find Mary, and Rotan would be worried by his absence. Paying scant notice to the scatter of shadows all around, he found his horse and rode out of camp. Again the lookout separated himself from the cedar.

'Two riders hide under the night,' he murmured.

Trav spoke acknowledgment and rode on. Within a mile, the mustang signaled danger with a wild tossing of its head. Two riders bore down upon him, and came in on either side.

'Parker? Been waiting for you. Didn't like

goin' too damn close to them cutthroats.'

There was enough starlight now for Trav to make out Pete and Brister.

'We'll take you back in,' Pete said. 'The judge wants a report.'

'I'll see him in the morning.'

'Nope. You'll see him tonight.'

'He said bring you straight to him, so you just ride with us and don't make any fuss,' Brister ordered. 'What'd you find out about them red cannibals? They gonna hit us?'

'You listen to what I'm telling you,' Trav said carefully. He had to make good on his promise of a wagonload of supplies for Blue Knife at sunup. 'You start a wagon of stuff to those Tonks at daylight. Plenty of beef, tobacco, a few bottles of whiskey for the chief's council. Anything else you got in the store. This is damned important if you want to keep them from butchering your town.'

'You can drive it yourself,' Pete retorted. 'Don't catch me at their camp in a wagon.'

'Then send it halfway out and leave it,' Trav argued. 'They'll come get it and take it the rest of the way.'

'Why not you?'

'I got other things to do.'

'The judge'll decide that.'

Brister added. 'He's all set up to hold court.' Trav detected the relish in the man's tone.

'Quite a thing,' Pete put in, as if speaking across to Brister, 'when the judge holds court.

Sumpin' to see.'

'Whiskey flows,' Brister said. 'For everybody. Everybody 'cept the poor bastard on trial.'

'I've seen 'em beg for whiskey,' Pete said.

'I've seen 'em beg for a bullet,' Brister added.

Smith was taking no chances that he would see Mary Jenkins tonight. That much was plain. He had to shake these two.

He kicked the mustang up a little, making it bear slightly to the right, toward Brister.

'Hey, what're you tryin'—'

Brister made a hand move toward his gun as Trav bent forward and reached his hand out in the darkness. His knife blade sliced across the bridle rein at the jaw of Brister's horse. Pete, in the same moment, plunged his own mount forward, to see what was happening. Trav whipped the knife to his left hand. Pete was in reach. Trav stroked once with the blade and the right rein in Pete's hand dangled loosely, severed from the bridle. In the next instant, Trav plastered himself low to the neck of the mustang and screamed a warwhoop in the night.

The horse muscles under him collected and the pony bellied low for a four-legged grab at space ahead. For a few terrified leaps, the frightened horses of Pete and Brister plunged alongside, but the commotion had erupted so suddenly that the two confused riders found

103

themselves fighting crazily just to regain a strangely lost control of their mounts. The Tonkawa trick had caught them napping. Gaps of space separated the three horses. With only one rein working to the bits of each outside horse, Pete and Brister yawed off right and left into the darkness like threshing sidewinders, cursing and fighting for management of horses seemingly gone loco.

Not until black distance hid his target did Brister take snap aim into the night. As his sixgun roared out a futile blast, Trav whacked his pony on the rump and stretched out flat. Riding with the horn in his chest, he made his run for the ghostly shapes of the settlement outlined in the hazy starlight.

CHAPTER EIGHT

Rotan stood with his thick legs peculiarly bent in a half crouch and stared across the room at Travis Parker. Hostility bristled out of him like quills on a porcupine. Trav shot a quick look at the whiskey bottle, and back to his partner. This was not drunkenness, though there might be a lot of whiskey behind it. Rotan's attitude seemed to combine a consuming dread and sudden personal dislike.

The swollen resentment in his expression sent a flash of alarm through Trav. *Partner* trouble? He tried to reject the idea.

Rotan blinked to cover the truth revealed— in his red-streaked eyes.

'Anything happen since I left?' Trav asked cautiously.

Rotan clenched and unclenched his big fists.

'Heard anything of Mary Jenkins?'

'Naw.' Rotan tightened his jaw knots.

'What's eatin' you?'

'You scared hell out of me!'

'It's nervous weather,' Trav shrugged. 'Those side stairs creak like a dry axle.'

He hadn't intended to startle his half-dozing sidekick when he slipped into the room. Rotan's demeanor, however, said something unexpected had developed that went deeper than the manner of Trav's stealthy entry. It had caused Rotan to shoot to his feet and halfway across the room, gun drawn, but it was not the main thing.

A jumble of things needed to be said or done, but Rotan's manner blocked them. Trav wanted to tell his partner quickly of the news he had wormed out of the Tonkawas. He was eager for Rotan to know that Denver Smith, as well as Jack Hinton, had been on the scene that night of the Territory bushwhack. He was anxious to get on the trail of Mary, to know if she was safe, and he wanted help in scheming a way to pump information from both her and Wilda Smith. But Rotan presented a strange, new problem that submerged the rest.

Trav closed the window through which he had crawled. He made a sign to Rotan that they should keep their voices down. The hour was somewhere halfway between midnight and first dawn, and the prairie night breeze cried a little in the big outside silence. In spite of his strange reception in the room, Trav became aware that he was famished. His glance worked over the place and found the remains of a meal in dishes on the dresser.

'You save anything for me?'

'Where'd you disappear to?' Rotan deanded. His words came out vicious and accusing, as if Trav had done him great wrong. Rotan held his rigid stance.

'What's eatin' you?' Trav asked again.

'You had me on edge the last three-four hours. Not knowing what had happened or anything. I don't cotton to this lunatic outfit.'

'Who does?' Trav tried a sympathetic grin but it didn't fit right and he gave it up. 'What the hell's the matter? You drunk?'

'Maybe drunk enough to play it smart,' Rotan retorted.

'Meaning?'

I've had a long time here to do a little thinkin'. Me, I'm the guy that killed Cabbo. The judge ain't gonna like me.'

Trav shot him a quick understanding grin that seemed more natural than his first try.

'Hell, Rotan, you're not any scareder than I am.'

Rotan shifted defensively but his glare held. Then the truth burst forth. 'I'm haulin' out while I got a whole hide.'

Trav looked him over speculatively, seeing not the man but the whole sorry tradition about partner trouble. Oldtimers claimed it always came to the best of friends if they fought the hard and lonely spaces too long. And they knew. Rotan was breaking out in his own form of cabin fever. Disconsolately, Trav recognized the symptoms, and his own inability to do anything about it.

He tore his eyes away from the older man because what he knew made his insides sick. Rotan was through.

For want of anything better to do, he limped to the dresser and rattled the dishes around. He uncovered a white crockery bowl and found that it contained a piece of fried beef, boiled potatoes, a wedge of cornbread.

Rotan began to lumber back and forth in the small confines of the room like a hurting animal. 'First, I thought they had you,' he complained. 'Either Smith's outfit or the Tonks. I damn near started to light out of here without waitin' to see.'

Trav remembered guiltily that retreat from Brazos Pass had been his own temptation only a little while ago. But he would not admit it to Rotan. The barrier was up and being nailed harder by both sides.

'Well, why didn't you?'

'I'm goin' to, right now!'

Trav chewed steadily and surveyed the stranger who had been his trail partner. He swallowed and said mildly, 'What you need is sleep. Smith's going to behave, long as he needs me to deal with those Tonkawas.'

Rotan spat out an obscenity of disagreement. 'I don't need the kind of sleep they're set to give us if we hang around. He ain't forgettin' it was me that shot Cabbo. They got a marshal that's a hired killer and they got a jail, and I'm not stayin' around to make the acquaintence of either.'

'Have you seen the judge since I left?'

Rotan shook his head. Then he flared up with a new displeasure. 'I saw *her!*'

'Wilda?'

'Yeah. His wife. Her that cottoned to you so quick.'

'When was this?'

'Middle of the night, and her askin' where you was and not much more clothes on than a squaw in a creek.' Rotan lumped in that extra portion of his general dislike for the situation and made a significant stare with his spooked eyes. 'You been with the Tonks or bedgroundin' with that filly?'

'Listen, mister—you itching to get out of trouble or start some? Which?'

'I asked you a question! You fool around that big bastard's private corral and you'll get us both killed!'

'Might be worth it,' Trav retorted, goaded now to baiting.

'You had you a Injin wife once, up there!' Rotan blasted. 'Whyn't you go back to her and the Tonks before this judge's woman beds you plumb to a coffin 'fore you're finished?'

Making one last steeled exertion for civility, Trav said, 'I had no wife up there. Never. I gave her back to Blue Knife the same day he gave her to me and damned near disrupted the whole tribe by doing it.'

'Well,' Rotan mumbled, 'anyhow that ain't gettin' us out of here.'

Trav forced himself to understand his partner's fear. Rotan had killed Cabbo. A few hours of thinking and a bottle of whiskey had convinced Rotan that the judge would never let him leave the settlement alive. Trav fought to keep an even tone. 'I've been at the Tonk camp,' he said. 'I think we can count on some help from Blue Knife.'

'You're squattin' on dynamite like it is, without stirrin' up more.'

Trav tore off a huge bite of the greasy beef and chewed angrily. The man across the room watched him for a long moment before giving an angry grunt of decision.

Rotan grabbed up the faded blanket, rolled his possessions in it and knotted the frayed tie ropes without a word. He tightened his gunbelt a notch and set his hat.

'I've wasted a whole damn year and more

followin' cold trails with you. I was out to find the Bradshaw money, and the man that stole it, same as you. Your man's dead and the hunt's over, far as I'm concerned. Me, I'm headin' back to civilization and a job.'

It shouldn't be this way. They had sidekicked so long together, dedicated to the same purpose of righting an old wrong. They had toiled side by side through so many dangers and setbacks. Now, with something big and important looming at hand, Rotan was pulling out. Trav restrained an angry impulse to tell Rotan to start riding and good riddance. Inside himself, he didn't mean it. Maybe if he explained a few things the bustup could be patched. It really was not Rotan's true nature to be spooked by one man or a hundred, red or white, or anything else that walked.

'I've been to see the Tonkawas,' Trav said quietly. 'It took a long time to let Blue Knife have his say. I'm sorry I left you here on edge, not knowing what was going on. But I think I've found out what we've been a long time looking for.'

As he spoke, Rotan moved impatiently toward the door, showing no pretense of caring. But Trav kept on.

'Now get Wilda Smith out of your craw and listen. I found two Tonks who heard Denver Smith's name called that night. Smith's name and Jack Hinton's. You hear that? They were *both* up there. If those Tonks are telling the truth, there were three men. One left when they had an argument. Headed out for Texas. The other two jumped me. All right, one of those murdered the other one, after they shot me. We can start counting the rattles on that.

'Jack Hinton was the one who rode for Texas, or he was the one who robbed me and killed the other man, which would make Denver Smith the one who rode for Texas. It had to be one way or the other because the third man's just a bleached-out skeleton in the Territory. Well, which one do we find living here at the end of creation like he had money, Hinton or Smith? Who got wind that we were making inquiries in this part of the country and all at once sent Ace Eckhart and Cabbo to kill Hinton? You say it's been a wild goose chase. I say, by God, we've found our man!'

In spite of all this, Rotan stayed stubbornly unimpressed.

Conscious of his tiredness all over, and of a return of the dull throb to his leg wound, Trav felt defeated. He walked to the window. To hell with Rotan. There were things to be done, and quickly, while the cloak of night still held. With a harshness he had not intended, he said, 'You hightail it if you want to. I'm going to cultivate Wilda Smith and I intend to get it out of her for certain whether Denver is the man I want. I'm finding Mary Jenkins, too, or Mary Hinton, if that's her name. Between the two of them I'm going to get my answers. I'm staying,

111

because there's just not any place for me to go back to until my name's cleared.'

Rotan bristled again. 'You're a damn fool!'

'I don't need you to tell me.'

'It may already be too late to get out. But I'm tryin' it, if I have to shoot my way loose from here!'

'Haul carcass, then.'

'Godamighty, boy,' Rotan rumbled pleadingly. 'We're outnumbered. I got sense enough to know when we're licked.'

He's got a yellow gut and he's had it all along and it's showing naked now, Trav thought. Two men can sidekick a long time, he reflected, without actually knowing what's inside one another. He felt a nausea of disappointment. Here was where the road forked for him and Rotan. Once split, the road would never come back together again.

He motioned toward the Winchester. 'You take it.'

Rotan caught up the old scarred repeater. He stood with the knotty blanket roll and rifle and they traded angry glares of finality. Trav grunted, 'Adios,' and turned. his back in the same moment that Rotan cautiously closed the door behind his exit.

Immediately, Trav dodged out of the lamplight. When his sight got fixed to the darkness, he tiptoed along the outside gallery toward the steep stairway to the ground. As he reached the bottom step, submerging into a

112

pond of muddy darkness, he heard a sound like a finger tapping on glass. He heard his name called. 'Trav!' Then again, 'Trav! Over here!'

He stopped, walked silently under the frame steps, feeling ahead with his hand for the corner window barely outlined in the adobe wall.

'Yes?'

'The window is open.'

He could make out her form now.

'Wilda? Are you alone?'

'Of course.' She gave a low tense laugh. 'I heard you when you went up. Come on!' she added impatiently. 'It's all right.' The word 'spider' bit into his mind, and the answer, 'fly.'

'Why don't you—come out? Let's go somewhere away from here.'

'There's not time.' She laughed softly and self-consciously. 'I've already waited for *hours*!'

He stooped through the open window and Wilda moved back, but when he straightened she was close to him. He could see that she wore something flowing and soft, and remembered Rotan's displeasure. Well, he was alone in this now. Rotan's ideas no longer counted. If this wasn't a trap of some kind, he was in luck. Being waylaid by her saved him the trouble of hunting her later for whatever information he could bait out of her. For a moment he knew the wild hope that perhaps Mary might be nearby, too, that possibly she

113

had taken refuge with Wilda. Then immediately he realized that would be unlikely, though he peered hard into the gloom, all around. The bed in the corner was empty.

Wilda had not moved away from him. He could feel her warm breath on his throat. 'Funny thing,' he said. 'I was just thinking about calling on you. A little late though, isn't it?'

'You were?' She sounded pleased. 'Then I'm glad I couldn't sleep.'

Her arms hung straight down her sides. Her face was lifted to him. He didn't like the darkness. He didn't like not being able to read her eyes, nor the risk of being here nor the feeling that he might have stepped into a trap he would have one hell of a time stepping out of. He almost wished Rotan was standing beside him, but he clipped off all thought of Rotan.

This woman could tell him things. He had to play every possibility. Fast, cautiously, disarmingly.

'Where's the judge? Holding court?'

'Oh, off somewhere. Never know where that man is. He's a night owl. It's just—us.'

'He ought to pay more attention to presiding over this court.'

'This court is not going to be around much longer. You'll help me to get out of here, won't you?'

'How do you know he'll not walk in here the next minute?'

'Because the door is locked. Don't act like a scared boy.'

'Maybe that's what I am.'

'You don't look it.'

'No? How do I look?'

'Like I like. Strong, calm outside, wild underneath. You know what the ugly one told me, your partner?'

'No telling.'

Wilda whispered teasingly, 'He said to lay off—that you had an Indian wife. That makes you all the more mysterious.'

'When do you want to strike out of here?'

'Tonight! Tomorrow—as soon as we can get away!'

'Will you answer a few questions for me?'

She moved slightly forward, until her clothing brushed him. Her lips came close for a mischievous whisper. 'Are you here just to ask questions?'

'It's a little risky for anything else.'

'Are you afraid? Aren't you a Ranger?'

'Who does the judge think I am?'

'Don't you trust me, Trav?' she pouted.

He stepped silently to the door, tested it, listened for sounds anywhere in the building. He came back, boots noiseless on the rug, and she turned toward him 'You answered my question,' she said.

'Men have been carried out on a shutter

who forgot to lock a married woman's door. I'll ask you again—where's the judge?'

'I never know! He's—well, all upset about things. The Indians out there. And about Cabbo. And—you. Oh, Trav, you must get away from here! Please! Leave this place while you can. And take me with you!'

'You really want to get out, don't you?'

'It's all I think about,' Wilda said fiercely. 'I'll do anything!'

She clutched his arm and Trav said, 'You told me you were willing to make a trade. Does that still go?'

Her fingers tightened possessively on his wrist. 'Yes! You're the first man I've seen in months I thought I could trust. Will you get me away?'

'You sound like you're a prisoner.'

'It's worse than that! I want to go where there are—*people*!'

He strained to catch noises in the outside night. He thought he heard footsteps somewhere in the building but could not be sure. He needed to hurry this.

'I want to ask you again,' he said carefully. 'Did you tell me the truth about Gus Jenkins? Mary's father. He was Jack Hinton?'

Her voice sounded impatient, as if this slant to the conversation was not what she had in mind. 'Of course. I had no reason to lie to you. He went by the name of Gus Jenkins.'

'Mary knows?'

116

'Yes, she knew it.' Wilda's tone turned brittle. 'You didn't need to mention *her* name!'

'Why did he do that? I want to know. Why was he living on that nester spread under another name? What did your husband have against him that he wanted him—'

'Don't say that!' Her words chopped harshly at him in the darkness.

His hand clamped hard on her soft upper arm through the thin silky covering of her robe. She struggled to pull back. Trav whispered, 'Don't say what? *Murdered?*'

She went limp to his touch. Her words came painfully from far down in her throat. 'I don't want to talk about that. I *won't* talk any more about anything!'

'It was your idea, that we make a trade.'

'I—I was thinking of something else.'

'You want to leave Brazos Pass. All right, you say I'm the only one can get you away. If you don't want to talk about Jack Hinton, then tell me where I'll find Mary. Why did Raffer take her away from somebody's house?'

'Why do you care?' Sullenly.

'Can't you just answer me?'

'I suppose you're more interested in Mary than in me! Well, you'll not get anywhere there! She's a little prude.'

'That's not what I'm talking about.'

His efforts to get information from her were just leading to a deadlock, he thought. After a long silence, Wilda moved out of his grasp with

117

a rustling whisper of her garments and looked through the window into the night.

'Mary Hinton is in jail.'

He stalked quickly to her. 'Why?'

'She's a suspect.' Wilda said indifferently. 'The judge ordered Raffer to lock her up.'

'Suspect in what?'

'The murder of a man named Ace Eckhart.'

Trav murmured in wonder: 'The self-appointed judge hires himself a town marshal, a sidewinder called Raffer, and runs the jail, the court, and all the people. Tell me, has your husband ever considered seceding from Texas?'

'He's a little—crazy, in a way,' Wilda confided. 'All his life, before, he was no more than a tramp rider. Now everything is grand ideas. Money. Show-off. He wants to lord it over the country, everybody. Including his wife.'

Trav stiffened. 'Before what? He was a tramp rider before what?'

She whirled on him with an explosion of indignation. 'You're using me!' she accused. 'Just pumping me! I offered—I had something else in mind. But all you want is talk, talk, *talk*!' Now she was a woman scorned. Trav sought quickly to placate her, but the moment for that already had passed. Wilda recklessly raised her voice. 'I could scream just once! And that would be the end of you, Mister Ranger!'

He chose to silence her in the only way that

118

seemed to fit his danger. He reached for her, caught her shoulder and jerked her forcibly to him. When she struggled, caught off guard, he only crushed her closer. Her hair smothered into his face as she tried to shake her head, gasping, 'No! No!' He engulfed the muscular strain of her resistence, and it subsided. He claimed the whole surrendering length of her body.

'No,' she said weakly.

'You mean no?'

'I mean—*yes!*'

Then her whisper ended caressingly in his name, gasped over and over. Her mouth came searching for his, and she clawed to him hungrily, struggling now to hold him closer. As her breasts flattened against his chest she slipped her arm down his side, and even in the engulfing storm of the moment he sensed that her hand had come to rest on the handle of his Colt. She pulled her mouth back enough to whisper, 'Take this off! I've sworn I'd never let a man love me while he had a sixgun on!'

His ears rang, shrill as a prairie storm, shutting out all sounds. But the storm had an ominous mutter, too, one that finally surfaced to his comprehension, and the ringing became underlaced with a thudding, marching sound that finally fixed itself in his brain as footsteps. Heavy and nearing.

He tore himself from her, and her hand dropped away from the Colt. Together, they strained to listen. Then, with a fear that sliced them apart, they moved hurriedly to the window.

'Quick!' Wilda whispered. 'Get out!'

'I'll see you again?'

'Yes! Yes! Tomorrow. I'll send word!'

He went through the opening. 'Can you keep him here for a while? Till sunup?'

'I can't promise. Go, now—quick!'

*　　*　　*

Mary sat in one chair in the bare room while Raffer gilded back and forth, badgering her with talk. The cold stone of the walls gave the room a dungeon-like cast in the gloom of a coal-oil lamp somewhere in the passageway outside the iron-grilled door. Judge Denver Smith's jail was in operation tonight.

Raffer flung his questions, sometimes whirling upon, Mary, twisting his mouth angrily. Once he thrust his hand under her chin and snapped her head up. But he was getting nowhere. Her only replies seemed to be spirited headshaking.

Trav, with an eye glued hard against a crack of light in the high barred window for the last several minutes, thought he could guess why Mary Hinton was being badgered by the judge's oily killer. The man had to determine the exact nature of Travis Parker's mission into the region.

Mary looked like somebody he had known a long time, a girl he had liked all his life. She looked brave and defiant, but haggared from the strain.

It was time to move on Raffer. He had seen all that he could take—Mary's tired eyes, the way she tried to hold her slight body rigid against Raffer's threats and baiting. It might have been going on for hours. Admiration for Mary welled up in him.

He had come to the jail, behind the long dark shadow of the judge's store, and had slipped silently to the place where he now stood beneath the window. In those few minutes he had heard no other sound but his own breathing and the occasional rustle of leaves in the pinoaks around him. Raffer's words did not penetrate the wall and closed window behind the shuttered bars. But that meant they could not hear him, either. He felt his way along the wall to the front corner to see what kind of door the squat stone building might have.

As his hand guided him to the sharp-edged stone corner, and around the turn, it encountered something soft. Not the stone, but a fabric feel, an alien substance that at first seemed a part of the building. He had touched a body.

The body came to life just as Trav rounded the corner. He saw the dark shadow move and take human form. A sleepily-muttered question in Mexican accompanied the dozing jail sentry into full awakening. Because he had not considered that Rafrer might have posted a lookout, Trav had no time to undo the damage. The man in the dark came unpropped from against the wall and his doze departed instantly. He tried to raise the rifle at his side. At such close quarters, the gun struck Trav a glancing blow on the arm as the sentry whipped it around. Trav grasped the barrel, shoving it away from him as he went for the man's throat with his right hand. In that moment of surprise he only knew that he had to keep the man from yelling.

His fingers dug deep into the bare yielding gullet, cutting off all sound but a choking groan. The man dropped the rifle, struggling, and tore at the choking hand with frenzied fingers. Trav hung on to his throat and drove his other fist smashing into the stomach. This brought the sentry's hands flying down to his new place of pain. Trav added his other hand to the throat. The sentry struggled, floundered, and slid downward, choking, with Trav falling hard upon him. The body under him kicked its legs like a dying horse, then went limp. Trav released his double-handed grip and started to rise.

The footstep sound behind him caught him halfway to his knees, trying vainly to twist aside. The fact that Raffer had put two lookouts on duty was the last full comprehension that came to him before the blasting red fire exploded in his head. Weakly, he tried to turn, to get up, to claw his way out of the black void. The arm above him rose high and came down again and that was all he saw. Fire broke into lava torrents of pain that roared down from a red swirling peak. The fiery sparks in his head exploded into blackness.

CHAPTER NINE

The guard in the passageway was a fat man with sleepy eyes and a half-moon of whiskers, sitting his life out watching the barred doors of the two cells. The lamp cast a wobbling light on the guard without diminishing the gloom of Trav's cell.

When he opened his eyes and sat erect on the floor, the guard looked at him dully. Trav steadied himself with fingers spread against the stone wall. He fought against the flames in his head where the man had clubbed him down. He staggered to the narrow door and caught the iron bars.

'Mary?'

No answer. Trav wondered if she had been released.

'Are you in there? Can you hear me?'

He was ready to give that up when he

caught the sliding sound of shoe leather on stone. Her voice, when it came, was surprisingly close.

'Trav? Trav Parker?'

'Mary! Are you all right?'

'Yes—I'm all right. I'm only sorry about what's happened to you.'

The guard blinked in annoyance. A growl came through the whiskers. 'Shut up!'

'Don't try to talk here, Trav.'

'Mind the pretty gal,' the guard advised. 'Go lay down.'

It would take something drastic to get the fat man up and to his feet, Trav thought.

'Can you still hear me, Mary? One question. Do you remember—what I wanted to know at your cabin? Do you, Mary? Would you tell me now?'

'Please—not now!'

'It may be my last—'

'No. Be careful, Trav.'

'Shut up!' the guard muttered.

'Mary—will the judge let you out of here? Are you going to be safe? Tell me.'

'I don't know, Trav. I think so.'

'What are they asking you? Is it about—the thing I came to your house asking? Your—'

'Damn yore blatherin'! I said lay down!' The guard shifted and halfway sat straight. He reached pudgy fingers to adjust the lamp wick.

'Where's Raffer?' Trav asked him.

'He'll be here. Don't you worry. So'll

124

Guerra.'

'Who's Guerra?'

'Man you near choked to death.'

'Trav!' Mary's voice was huskily urgent. 'If you get a chance, just any kind of a chance—please go! Leave here. It's the most I can do for you. just to tell you—leave, if you get even one little chance.'

He barely heard her. A dove had called twice from somewhere outside. Soft, slow, and mournful. With three of the little short, fading low notes at the end, each time. He sucked in a deep breath.

'What's your name?' he asked the guard.

The guard made a puzzled frown. 'Who'n hell wants to know?'

'Thought I'd seen you somewhere.'

'Yeah? Well, it's Bumble. You don't like it, go lay down and shut up.'

'Bumble?' Trav raised his voice loud in surprise. 'I've heard that name. Bumble-Bumble.'

'Yeah. Like a damn bee. And I'm gonna sting yore noggin harder'n Brister did if you don't quit jawin'.'

Trav raised his voice even louder. 'His name is Bumble, Mary! You know Bumble?' On the last word, he turned his head to face the outside door of the hallway.

Mary spoke sharply. 'Don't push him, Trav! You don't know them!'

He heard the dove call. Such an innocent

125

sound. The gray gloom in the window had lightened a little. It couldn't be, he argued to himself. The muted notes were in his throbbing head.

A heavy hand rattled the barred door out of sight at the end of the passageway. A rough voice called with careless authority,

'Bumble! Hey, Bumble! You awake?'

The guard brought his chair sharply down to its front legs and began the motions of collecting himself to his feet.

'Hell, yes, I'm awake. All this mouthin'—'

'Raffer sent me to relieve you.'

'Damn high time.' Bumble shuffled down the hallway and out of sight. On his toes, straining, Trav heard the swing of iron hinges.

Maybe I'm dreaming, he thought.

Bumble's outsized rear section appeared as a shadow on the wall, kept coming. The shadow's arms were up. A sixgun seemed to protrude from Bumble's mammoth belly, handle-end first, and on the handle end, a fist. Trav knew the fist, and the arm, every old detail. Bumble kept walking backward, hands thrust high, and the aim with the gun became a shoulder. The shadowy figure marched Bumble backward, full into the lamp light. Trav could only hold on to the bars, wetting his lips, afraid to try to speak because words were soggy lumps in his throat. The face that seemed to be propelling Bumble down the passage belonged to the ugliest man in Texas.

And it looked plumb beautiful.

The sixgun jabbed the fat belly.

'Your chair.' Rotan pointed. 'Have a sit.'

Bumble sat. It was the best thing he did and he kept stretching his hands for the roof while Rotan took his keys.

'Don't go nowhere,' Rotan said. He then nodded politely to Trav. 'Her first. If you don't mind. Ladies—'

'I don't mind a damn thing,' Trav assured him.

Rotan lumbered unhurriedly to the adjoining cell door. The key worked. The door squeaked open.

Mary came into Trav's line of vision. Her worried smile flashed to him, then vanished. She stood trying to straighten the stray ends of her hair, while Rotan worked the key again.

'You speakin' to me?' Rotan mumbled.

'I just want to say—' Trav couldn't think of a way to put it.

Rotan understood. 'Two fools like us ought not to talk this early in the morning.'

Trav grinned tightly at his partner. The old, creviced features wrinkled a little in a responding grin. Rotan said, 'Bumble will look better in that cell. Out yonder, back of the store, somebody's hitchin' a team to a wagon. Wagon loaded with sides of beef and some stuff. Been spyin' a little. Wagon's got a cover on it. Good place for a girl.'

Trav nodded. 'For the Tonk camp.'

He spotted his gunbelt, holster and Colt hanging on the wall of the corridor. He retrieved it, then directed Bumble into the cell and locked the door.

'What do you want to do?' he asked Mary. 'Where do you want to go?'

'I don't know.'

'Then you'll go with me.'

She started to speak, and couldn't. He felt a surge of compassion. Poor little nester girl. She had no place to turn, nobody to go to, and now she must place herself in his hands because of her transparent helplessness to do anything else. She managed to move her chin a fraction, indicating agreement. Unashamedly, she touched her forefinger to the corner of each eye.

'Would you like to hide somewhere in the village, Mary? Wilda Smith—would she help you?'

Her breath came out in a long sigh. 'Not Wilda. Not her.'

Trav moved to the door, still half open, the way Bumble had left it when he had heard Rotan call his name. The sky had lightened. The settlement would be astir in no time. The people forted in the houses probably were already at the windows with guns ready for threat of Indian attack.

'How about you?' he demanded of Rotan.

'I'm givin' up ramroddin', as of now.' His partner grinned sheepishly. 'I done my little

128

stunt. Hope I halfway made up for bein' a damn fool.'

'How far'd you get?'

'Bout a mile. Turned around right in the middle of a high lope, without the horse's feet touchin' ground. It just hit me—what'n hell am I doin', ridin' off south by myself? Feel like a polecat. Reckon you know that. Traced some commotion down to this place and here I am.'

Trav dug a hand into the heavy shoulder. 'You're no polecat. You're a dove. You coming with me?'

'Where?'

'The Tonk camp. Nowhere else to go.'

'You want me to?'

'Would you listen to another idea?'

'Yep. Done enough talkin' last night to last me a lifetime.'

'That's forgotten.' Trav lowered his voice so that his words would not carry to Bumble. 'There's a detachment of Rangers at Fort Belknap. Or was. That's where the North Fork of the Brazos runs into the main stream. There should be a man in charge there named Captain Small. It's three days' hard riding. You willing to try it?'

'I don't like ridin' off leavin' you in a fix,' Rotan protested. 'I done that once too many times, this mornin'.'

'This is different. This is our only chance, the way I see it. If you can find him—if Captain Small will listen—give him this message for me. You tell him that I'm here, that I think I've found the answer to why Texas is bogged down at the Brazos, that this job needs the Rangers. You tell him the Union cavalry at Fort Concho is pigheaded blind to what's up here—no help out of that barracks. They're content to just watch the Comanche trails into Mexico, that's all. You'll just have to tell him what we've found and make it stick. If they want to put a stop to this comanchero trade, tell him we've found the champion comanchero of them all up here above the Cap Rock. And tell him this. Tell him he can open a country half as big as the rest of Texas while the Yankee Army is twiddlin' its thumbs, if he wants to. I think he'll listen to you.'

Rotan nodded. 'You don't have to worry about how I'll lay it on. Anything else?'

'You might say to Captain Small that if my name doesn't mean anything to him—' His words thickened a little but he couldn't help it. 'Tell Captain Small that I said—that under the same circumstances, even like everything is—that Shamrock Parker would have come. Just to find out.'

Trav saw his hat on the floor and picked it up. Pushing between the silent pair, he made a cautious survey from the door. Without turning, he spoke to Rotan. 'Your mount handy?'

'Back in the trees. I can get to him all right.'

'Good luck. That dove call was like music to

me—partner. Mary, you wait here.'

He stepped from the jail doorway, onto the dew-soaked grassy path, and walked rapidly toward the back of the store where the outlines of a covered wagon showed in the dawn light. As he came around the team, a man straightened to face him with squinting inquiry. Trav asked briskly, 'You the one driving out the supplies to the Tonks?'

'That's me.' The gaunt features showed no pleasure. 'My hard luck for knowin' a little Tonkawa language. Why?'

'I'm to relieve you. The judge's orders.'

For a moment, the driver showed relief and Trav began to think his bluff had succeeded. Then, as they momentarily faced each other, slow suspicion seeped back to the driver's expression. He backed off.

'Ain't you the feller I heard they had in jail?'

He might have talked the man into peaceful acceptance of the situation, even then. But the opportunity came apart when a high-pitched squawl of warning sounded from the jail window. Bumble had found his voice.

Trav whirled back in time to see the driver start a slow reach for his gun. The Colt was already clearing its holster within a fisted hand that fumbled a little from the driver's mental uncertainty. Trav slapped up his own Colt and fired once.

The other sixgun went spinning to the ground like a red-hot thing flung from burned fingers. The driver jerked his hand hard to his chest. He stared at his bloody knuckles. Then Trav closed with him in one steel-coired spring, and the side of his Colt smashed hard against the man's head above the ear. The driver shuddered over his full gaunt length and sagged to the ground.

Behind Trav, at the cell window, Bumble loosed another long-drawn wail. Trav knew glumly that he had misfigured Bumble.

He jumped to the wagon seat, caught up the reins, and savagely backed the team in a seesawing course to the jail doorway behind him.

'Climb over the tailgate,' he called.

In a moment Mary's voice said, quite near, 'I'm in.'

'Keep low on the floor. Get something between you and the opening.'

He popped the slack end of the lines to the rumps of the buckskin pair. They made a jumping start and the rig went rattling out to the road. The ornate front of the Brazos Palace rushed toward Trav in a gray smear of daylight. He saw the man with a rifle burst from the doorway. Back at the jail, a yell drifted high. Somewhere a gun cracked out a quick warning staccato of shots. The man in front of the Palace ran into the street, raising his rifle as he came, and the wagon tore down upon him. He appeared uncertain in the way he brought the rifle to a bead, hesitating, and then Trav fired at close range as the wagon careened past.

The rifleman jumped, flung his weapon aside, and caught at his shoulder. The buckskin team panicked into a full run and Trav had to fight the lines for control. As the team took the curve of the street in an explosion of dust, Trav threw a backward glance and saw the man at the Palace grabbing the rifle out of the dirt. The snap shot he made clipped the sand ahead and to the left, and the second bullet rang against steel somewhere at the back of the wagon.

Then the wagon rounded the curve in the road and a house cut it off as a target. Trav breathed with relief as the last shadowy house floated past. The running team tore into the southern sweeps of the open prairie.

In the distant first streaks of daylight he sighted a spectacular snaking movement on the grassy floor of the plain. A mile to the east of the distant stand of trees, Blue Knife had his warriors in a running formation of mounted flow and color. They came wheeling and maneuvering in assault tactics copied long ago from their savage tormentors, the Comanches and Kiowas. Straight toward this fluid display Trav headed the team which had begun to slow after their first frenzied run.

'Are you all right back there?'

Her voice was low, almost at his back. 'Trav, they're coming behind us. Some men on

133

horses.'

He risked a backward glance, straining from the edge of the seat to peer beyond the wagon cover. There seemed to be five or six riders, scattered dots of pursuit, just clearing the fringe of the settlement. Ahead, he saw the feathered Tonkawas beginning a full-run charge upon him.

The sight of the Indians must have been more spine-chilling to Mary than the pursuit from the town. 'Will they attack us, you think?'

They would stampede the team, he muttered angrily. At the rate they were coming the crazy Tonks would have their supplies scattered over half the prairie, likely with Mary and himself dragged along in a sorry mess inside an overturned wagon.

'Hang on to something!' he yelled above the wagon rattle.

A half-mile away, the warriors changed their course. Trav fought the team's frightened shenanigans and worked them down to a trot. The Tonkawas curled past, changed directions, and then went on, raising dust and yells, fullforce toward the pursuing horsemen.

Trav looked back. In a matter of seconds, the bunched-up white riders turned tail and streaked back toward the settlement. Sight of the hundred charging Tonkawas had been too much for them.

Pulling up at the edge of the camp in the grove, Trav helped Mary to the ground. Fear stretched like a second skin over the thin face which she raised to him.

'What you need is sleep.' He managed a reassuring grin. 'Same as me. You mind sleeping in a Tonk chief's hide *tipi*?'

Her shoulders lowered in indifference, as if her last strength for decision had ebbed. Blue Knife rode up, alone. Trav spoke to him, gesturing to the wagon, and then to the tent. Blue Knife made a sign and rode away, and Trav guided Mary deeper into the trees. As he turned back, he saw Blue Knife riding to meet his warriors who were now charging upon the wagon. Denver Smith's first installment of supplies would hold them for a while. He guided Mary to the *tipi* opening. Inside, he indicated a blanket for her, turned his back, rolled up in the other blanket, and quickly passed into the deep oblivion of dead-tired sleep.

*   *   *

The dim light seeped into the hide tent where the white man and the white girl were sleeping off their weariness. Awakening first, Trav propped on his elbow and peered across the space of the *tipi*. A Tonkawa blanket outlined the drawn-up curve of Mary's small body.

Mary stirred slightly. She caught him looking at her. Remembrance flooded into her sleep-relaxed face. She pulled the blanket

135

tighter to her throat.

'Blue Knife is lending us his house.' He made a careless motion to the hide walls. 'Mary, will you answer some questions for me now?'

She huddled inside the covering of the blanket. 'What do you want to know?'

'What was Raffer trying to get out of you? Why did they take you to the jail?'

'The judge!' Her eyes clenched shut, opened again. Her mouth tightened in bitterness.

'What were they really trying to get out of you?'

'About you, Trav. Who you were. Why you'd come here, what my father had told you. Things like that, over and over.'

'What did you say?'

'Just that I didn't know.'

'Why was your father using that Jenkins name? Who is Denver Smith, and what did he have against your father.

He saw the pain, the way she stiffened, but he finished: 'Why did he have Cabbo kill your father?'

Her suspicion rose between them like a barrier. Through the wall of distrust her voice came cautiously. 'You said yesterday at our cabin—that there was something more. Something good and *dirty*.' She paused. 'About the trouble, all that happened to you.'

He looked straight into her eyes, not four

feet away. 'You ever hear of being drummed out of the Army? Well, it was something like that. Only this was a Ranger company and not many of them spoke to me when I left.'

'But couldn't you *explain* to them?' Her tone was huskily sympathetic. Then it dawned on him that he had helped build this barrier of mistrust. He was not satisfying her own curiosity any more than she was satisfying his. If he told this girl the plain truth, spread it out before her like a blanket on the grass, maybe she would do the same.

'It was like this,' he said, trying to determine the place where his troubles had their beginning. 'Bradshaw started it. He came to my captain and asked him to assign me to ride to Abilene to bring back his herd money. He had contracted with Jack Hinton to move the herd up. Maybe you knew about that. But he wanted a Ranger to bring the money back, and I hope I'm not hurting your feelings. It was the way Bradshaw wanted it.'

'It was his privilege,' Mary said. 'But it hurt my father. Hurt him not to be trusted. I never knew much about it, though. So the Rangers sent you?'

'They couldn't, officially. They couldn't detach a man and send him halfway across the world on a private errand for somebody, to bring a big cattleman's money back from another state. So Captain Small tried to do this for Bradshaw by a paper manipulation that put

137

me on leave. He wanted to accommodate Bradshaw, you understand, and he figured to do it that way to dodge regulations. So when I went north, I wasn't under official orders. I was on leave of absence. Small and Bradshaw had been friends of my father, Shamrock Parker. He had been a Ranger, and maybe that's why they picked me. Well, I got the money in Abilene. I never saw your—never saw the man who took the cattle up, nor any of the trail crew. The bank paid over the sixty thousand to me on Bradshaw's order and I headed south. Wasn't long before I knew I was being followed.'

He stopped there. Mary raised herself on her elbow, too, so their eyes met on a level. She said, 'You don't have to tell about the ambush if you don't want to.'

'Well, I'll just say this—I was shot up pretty bad. First I thought I was dying and didn't care much. Not with the money gone. The Tonks pulled me through. I lived in their village a long time. A year, way I figure it. They taught me a lot about Indians and I guess I taught them a little about white men's ways. I'll skip that. One day when I had a chance I pulled out. You want to know what happened when I got back to Texas?'

'Not if it troubles you too much to tell.'

'Well, it was a whole hell-fire of trouble, I can tell you that. Bradshaw was ruined and he killed himself. His relatives made plenty of

138

trouble over it. The word leaked out that the Rangers had sent me, and that I had made off with the money. That put Captain Small in a bad spot with headquarters. All kind of rumors went around, and even the governor took a hand in it by then. Somebody's hide had to be nailed up. I don't think the Ranger headquarters knows to this day whether I lied or not. But that's a military outfit and the military's not accustomed to being the goat in a tight place, if they can pass the buck.

'So they did the only thing they could to clear their skirts. They had a full-grown scandal on their hands and everybody was trying to save his own neck. They kicked me out with a dishonorable discharge and told me I was damned lucky not to be tried as a criminal. The Bradshaw heirs wanted to hang me. Now that's what I rode back to from the Tonks, and that's what put me on the trail of Jack Hinton for all these months. Whoever pulled that ambush owes me a look at him over the sight of this Colt.'

She said, 'I am not blaming you, Trav. Not blaming you for anything. Something like this had to happen, I think.'

He seized at this indication of her understanding. 'Then will you tell me now—the things I need to know?'

Whatever she might have said was cut off by moccasin shuffles at the opening. A painted face showed, a long dark arm shoved through.

Mary cringed close to her cover as Trav whirled. It was only a Tonk buck bringing food to them. The buck grunted, spoke guttural words, made a motion to include them both, and withdrew.

'What did he say?' Mary asked.

'He thinks you're my squaw.'

He noticed the small tint of color go to her olive cheeks. The deep blue depths of her eyes contained a tiny smile.

Her next words, murmured with a trace of timidity, startled him. 'Trav,' she asked, glance averted, 'who is Bee-lah?'

He swallowed hard on a barely-chewed bite of beef. 'Why do you ask that?'

'You said her name when you were asleep.'

'How do you know it was a *her*?'

'Because. The way you said it.'

That's the way a woman makes her own logic as she goes along, he thought. 'What else did I say?'

Her reply didn't come at once, but rather stayed in hiding and then cautiously peeked out in words like a chipmunk nosing up from a pile of leaves. 'You said my name.'

'I said just "Mary"?'

'You said "Mary." Then you said something I didn't understand. It sounded like "twenty ponies."'

He tried to see her more clearly in the gloom, to see if he actually had detected a small note of hidden mischief. Her eyes

140

showed nothing but controlled blankness. She added flatly, 'I know a little something about Tonkawas.'

'That lick on my head,' he managed to mumble. 'Nightmares. The man hit me pretty hard.'

He tried to eat again. After a minute, the voice came shyly from the other blanket. 'You haven't said who Beelah was.'

This questioning business had meandered clear off the trail. A man couldn't drag a thing out of her against her wishes. And she was as tenacious with her own tracking of fact as a badger on a moonlight forage.

Because she flustered him, he said, 'You haven't told me anything, either. How much longer until we begin to trust one another?'

Immediately he was sorry. He had been as gruff as an old buffalo, which was not what he had intended. The beef chunks on the hot stone slab sent up a high, gamy odor. No further word issued from the small blanketed huddle. He changed positions until he saw Mary's eyes reflecting the particles of stray sunlight seeping in. Her face was shadowed and a little afraid. Afraid of this day, perhaps, of people white and red, and of the world around. But he saw courage, too, as if some steely strength inside her, some secret reserve for meeting fear, was struggling to overcome whatever she had to face.

The space between them closed to nothing

as he twisted his shoulders in a slide across the grass-tufted floor. His body stretched to the small blanketed lump of her, and his arm reached across her shoulder. She did not shrink to his touch, nor could he tell if she breathed at all. He kissed her, once, gently.

Her lips did not respond. He drew back to his own place, his mind in a flutter of confusion. The feel of her mouth remained warm on his. A disturbance at the opening rescued him from the jumble of words from which he was trying to choose the right ones to say to her.

He recognized the paint-daubed ugliness of Fox One-Eye. Fox did not come all the way in, but poked his tattooed shoulders through the opening, and a whiskey smell with it, and grunted Tonkawa words. His jabber ended with a leering grin and a hand gesture toward Mary, and Trav was glad that she did not understand Tonk. He shot an angry reply at the one-eyed warrior. Fox flung a folded paper at him and sullenly withdrew. Mary must have guessed at the Indian's implication for she did not ask the obvious question. Instead, she watched unspeaking as Trav picked up the paper, unfolded the note and read the words penciled in a feminine hand:

I will get away tonight and meet you both at Mary's cabin. Then all three of us can escape together. Please do this, Trav! It is for the

sake of you both—you and Mary. Your
only chance.   Wilda

He read it aloud to Mary. 'Fox said another
wagon of supplies came out at noon. The
driver brought Wilda's note.'

After that, they sat silent for a few minutes,
and his decision formed. With Mary's safety at
stake, this seemed to be his only course. Wilda
would know of their danger better than
anyone. As she had said, it was their only
chance. Certainly, he could no longer oppose
the judge's forces with Mary on his hands.

'What do you think?' he asked her. 'Is Wilda
to be trusted in this?'

She nodded thoughtfully. 'Yes, in this, I
think. Or she wouldn't have risked getting the
note smuggled to us by the wagon driver. She
wants to get away, more than anything. And
what else is there for us to do?'

It would mean failure in his long hunt. But
the danger stood clear before him. A man
sometimes came to the end of a trail, a place
where he had to give up in defeat.

Or did he?

Maybe there was another way. He wanted
more than anything to have a look at the
judge's ranch house somewhere to the west.
Why not ride with Mary to the Gus Jenkins
nester shack, meet Wilda there, and send the
two women on their way eastward toward
civilization and out of the judge's reach? Then

he could circle back alone and find his way to the Denver Smith cattle spread. He owed it to himself to try a final time to dig out the proof of the man's identity.

He nodded his agreement. 'I can't let you fall into the judge's hands again, Mary.'

'I know,' she whispered fearfully. 'It's too late to cope with him now. Because I've been with you.'

'He'd be afraid of what you might have told me?'

'Of course.'

Too quickly, he shot the question again. 'Who is he, Mary?'

'Please!' She turned away. 'Let's ride for my house, now. To meet Wilda, to get out of this country. All of us!'

With his jaw hard set, he motioned her to the opening.

'When we go to get horses out here, just walk close behind me. Don't look right or left. If they mix some English into what they may start jabbering about us, don't hear that, either.'

Her quick intuition silenced her, clamping down upon the curious 'Why?' he almost could see form on her lips. She managed a thin smile. Demurely, she stood aside as a squaw would have done, to permit him to walk first from Blue Knife's shelter into the sun-lighted maze of staring painted faces.

CHAPTER TEN

They rode southeast in the late afternoon. With enough distance between them and Brazos Pass, he drifted their course north again in, into the Brazos roughs, on through the early hours of night. Now they were back in the same country they had crossed only yesterday, going to the settlement with the nester, Gus Jenkins, alive and on the verge of talking. And tonight the land seemed even more forbidding and lonely.

The strenuous ride gave no opportunity for conversation, and Trav's disappointment persisted, a heavy weight within him. Just a few feet beyond his reach, this tight-mouthed girl held at least a part of the answer he needed locked inside her.

They walked the weary Indian ponies across the last dry creek, up the brushy ridge. They looked down upon the dark nester shack that had been Mary's home.

Trav worked on his plan to send the two women away to safety. He would give the horses a few hours' rest. He decided that he should ride with them the first day. This would take them across the wilds of the upper Brazos. Then he would direct them on a route that would eventually bring them into Fort Belknap. By then, he would be well on his way over the trail back—the same hard route to ride again, back across the roughs, to the sea of grassy plains. Back to the land west of the settlement, in search of the Denver Smith place. If only the Tonks would hold the men inside the settlement for a few more days. That was about all the luck he could ask.

And as for Mary Hinton and the runaway wife of Denver Smith—tomorrow would be the last he'd see of them, likely.

'Pull up here a minute,' he said.

Mary brought her pony alongside.

'Anything you want to tell me, Mary? Before we see Wilda?'

She shook her head. 'But I'd like to see her first. Alone.'

He could think of no reason for that, but it didn't matter. She was not going to tell him anything, now or ever.

'All right. There's a horse tied at the porch. She made it. Go ahead and see her. I'll pen these mounts, and hers.'

'May I light a lamp?'

'Yes. Hang some blankets or something over the windows.'

As Mary dismounted in front of the dark cabin, he took her reins and headed for the pole corral. When he returned, walking toward the house, the window cracks showed yellow traces of lamplight. He meant next to take Wilda's horse, still saddled, to the pen. The horses would have to be fed and watered. He hesitated, and decided to tell the girls to make the window hangings blot out the trace of the light inside. He walked upon the porch, knocked lightly, swung the door and stepped inside.

Raffer stood spread-legged at the far end of the room, holding his two sixguns leveled.

'Come in, Ranger,' Raffer said.

Trav shot a look to one side. He saw Mary, standing white-faced, and Wilda, sitting in a dejected slump.

Raffer's mouth twisted. 'Reach high, Parker.'

The judge's lawman tightened his fingers on both triggers. Trav reached high.

'A trap.' He spoke through dry lips.

'No.' Wilda shook her head. Defeat sagged her voice. 'He followed me.'

'The judge likes for me to keep an eye on you, ma'am.' Raffer smirked.

Wilda moaned. 'He's taking us back. I've tried bribery, everything.'

'You take his gun off him.' Raffer spoke to Mary. 'Don't walk between us.'

Trav watched Mary start reluctantly toward him. Raffer muttered, 'He wants you alive.'

Trav caught the stiffened movement of Wilda's hooted legs. A message flashed from her narrow eyes. The door still yawned open to the darkness behind him. His own leg muscles tensed.

'The judge wants me alive, too,' Wilda said,

147

and turned languidly to Raffer. Then she shot to her feet with wildcat swiftness and flung herself upon Raffer with a fury that sent him stumbling off balance. Her arms struck down viciously upon Raffer's two extended guns as she grappled with him. She swarmed upon the little killer, fighting like a man. Trav churned his feet backward. He stumbled through the opening, yanking the door closed behind him, vaulted to the saddle of Wilda's horse and jerked the rein hitch loose. He spurred the animal into the dark yard. He sent the horse crashing through the darkness, headed for the brush. The first shot finally came.

Raffer's bullet whistled to one side, and then there was no target for Rafrer except the hoofbeats of the running horse, fading into the night.

But Trav's first satisfaction in escape shortly turned to the bitterness of self-accusation. As he rode deeper into the night, the fact gnawed at him that he had deserted Mary. Wilda, no doubt, could take care of herself. She had known that Raffer was not going to pull a trigger on Denver Smith's wife. But he had left Mary to be returned to the judge. Once he slowed the horse and considered turning back. And as quickly, he abandoned the idea. It would be foolhardy. He had to leave the two women. He could help them only if he stayed free and unfettered. If he went back for a gunfight with Raffer the man would have two living shields.

He kept to the roughs until daylight, then screened the horse in a cedar clump and dozed fitfully off and on through the day. At sundown he rode westward again. This time he swung north, keeping to cover, because he could not know whether the judge would send reinforcements to join Raffer. If so, once they learned that Trav Parker had escaped the little gunman, they might begin combing the country. As he rode he became sleepy again, but the sleepiness suddenly jolted into blood-pounding wakefulness as he caught sight of the column of smoke skylighted on a star-lit ridge.

Half an hour later he emerged afoot at the clearing where the air hung heavy with fire smell. The house might have been Drain's, or some other nester place. But it was a house no longer; nothing but charred, smoldering lumber and ashes. The skeleton silhouette of the rock chimney poked up crookedly in the night. Trav scouted the fringes of the clearing, and found the horse pen gate open, the pen empty.

He retraced his way to the mount hidden in the saplings, and rode off with his nerves raw and stinging the back of his neck. He worked all the speed he could get out of Wilda's big-muscled roan, and made the Tonkawa camp before sunup. In Blue Knife's tent he confronted the old chief with a terse question.

'Have the Tonkawa warriors made a night

raid?'

When Blue Knife understood his question, he replied in the negative.

'Then your old enemies are somewhere in this country,' Trav told him bluntly.

Blue Knife stared, long and hard. His old eyes showed that he was trying to deny to himself the dismaying truth.

Trav nodded. 'They're on the raid. Comanches.'

The Tonkawas stayed close to the camp grove through the following day. Once, they made the pretense of a charge upon the settlement. But he knew their eyes were fearfully cast to all the distant country. Word swept their ranks that the Comanches had crossed the Brazos.

Trav rested through the day with fitful impatience, and before dawn of the following morning he could no longer endure his restlessness. Mary Hinton was somewhere there in the distant village. He could think of no way to help her without risking his own capture. But he could make one more gamble for a contact with the nesters, an appeal to them to help Mary, to give her assistance somehow.

It was not yet daylight when he rode from the Tonkawa camp, first west, and then into the outskirts of Brazos Pass from the north. He left his horse and went on afoot toward the lamp-lighted windows of Rigsby's house.

*   *   *

At the Brazos Palace, in the early evening of the day after Raffer had brought back the two women, Wilda Smith emerged purposefully from her room. She wore riding clothes. She walked down the corridor to the doorway of the small room at the end of the balcony. Denver Smith had posted a guard there over his prisoner, Mary Hinton. Wilda gave the man a look of haughty indifference.

'I'm calling on your prisoner,' she informed him.

The man drew aside. Wilda opened the door, enteredy and closed it behind her.

For a long moment, the two women stared at each other—the judge's prisoner and the judge's wife. Mary stood unmoving at the foot of the iron bed.

'They buried him yesterday afternoon,' Wilda murmured. 'The nesters did, that is. They read the service, everything proper. I thought you'd want to know.'

She was near enough to touch Mary's arm. A tender, tentative gesture. Mary looked impersonally into the wet green eyes of Wilda Smith. Wilda's painted lips trembled.

'He was a righteous man,' she said.

Mary drew back. 'Our father? You used to say he was a hard man.'

'He was hard with me, yes.'

151

'But you made your decision,' Mary said slowly. She glanced away, hopelessly, at the walls, anywhere but at her sister. 'I don't think anything could ever really change you. Not even death.'

For a moment, Wilda gave way to a seizure of emotion. She dabbed clumsily at the half-formed tears. That passed, and she moved nervously about in the small room.

'You say he was a hard man,' Mary told her. 'Well, the world knows you as a hard woman. You turned into something he never intended, could never understand. Yet he wouldn't give up. He always hoped, I guess. Living up here as we did, just so he could sometimes see you. He was thinking of Mother, I know. It was a debt he owed her and he tried to pay it the best way he could.'

Wilda painstakingly tucked in a loosened wisp of hair. Through a hairpin held in her teeth she said carelessly, 'Don't get pious with me. I'm working on Denver to turn you loose.'

Mary's eyes blazed. 'Vicious! You were born vicious! And bad!'

This brought a brittle laugh from the older woman. 'I wasn't going to be a poor man's brat all my life.'

'He never understood you. I feel that I almost never knew you.'

Wilda shrugged. 'The bright lights were horn in my blood, I guess. You and I were so different. When Mother went back to the footlights it took us a million miles away from your life. She took me, he took you. I guess each of us got the parent she wanted. And that was that. You've had your life and you're welcome to it. We had ours and I grew up the way I wanted.'

Mary Hinton drew her small body into a taut shell of solitude as if removing herself physically distant from Wilda Smith. 'You were never like a sister to me,' she said.

'Then there's no love lost.'

'How many men have had to pay with their lives, as he did? So that you and Denver Smith could live like lords?'

'It wasn't the way I thought it would be,' Wilda retorted harshly. 'But now I'm in it and the time passed long ago when I could turn back.'

'You're his prisoner, too,' Mary declared, almost triumphantly. 'Just as much so as all the little people out here.'

Wilda shrugged. 'Maybe so, maybe not. We'll see about that. I've still got an axe over his thick neck and he knows it. You know it. I've got something safe in writing somewhere and nothing is going to happen to me! Well, keep your nose clean, nester gal. I don't think Denver would harm you, not as long as that black-listed Ranger is on the loose. But be careful.'

Then she moved quickly across to Mary and whispered in her ear: 'Take this. Try to slip out

153

before daylight. Go to Rigsby's.' She pressed a key into Mary's hand and departed.

Wilda had thought the judge would be out very late, this night. But he came to their room earlier than she expected. Denver fastened the door behind him, not turning his back to her. The lumpy corners of his thick face twitched at the points of his close-clipped mustache.

'You forgot my flower today.' He knocked lightly on his empty lapel with a mighty fist. Wilda froze. He took a few steps into the room, his light-footed movements silent on the rug. 'Maybe I ought to have you arrested for neglectin' your duty.'

The whiskey odor snaked over the room. Wilda, as if recognizing a sign, exclaimed, 'Please, you're not planning to hold court tonight?' The statement that started angrily ended in a questioning plea. 'Not after all that's happened?'

'What's the matter? Something upset you?'

'Everything's upset me!'

'I can see.' His eyes burned brighter. 'You're so upset you forgot and put on riding clothes again to go to bed in. Wasn't that one little ride enough?' He drifted a look over her whipcord pants and open-throated shirt. 'I might just hold court, after all.'

'Who?' Wilda breathed.

'Her.'

'Mary?'

'You know, I've always hated the smart

154

ones. The ones that think they've got me fooled.'

'Who thinks they've got you fooled. Denver?' She tried to make her voice light and it came out false and she knew he was not deceived. Shrilly she said, 'With all those Indians out there and the nesters in town, it's no time to hold a drunken orgy of a trial downstairs and you know it! One more screaming night of that is more than I can stand.'

'She wouldn't scream very loud. She's a brave Hinton. Real smart. Hobnobs with the young Ranger. Like you'd do if you had a chance.'

He sauntered a step or two toward her. Nervously, she rubbed at the open collar of her shirt.

'As soon as we get rid of the Tonks,' the judge mumbled. 'Just as soon as those cannibals are gone.'

'But not tonight!' she nodded quickly, smiling approval. 'I'm so glad you won't have a court tonight.'

'I'd like to hold court over that Parker. He wouldn't be so handsome after a trial. Wouldn't interest you so much, eh?'

She flung an indignant denial of interest in Trav Parker.

He extended a heavy hand and patted her shoulder. His eyes burned strangely and his whiskey sweat made a warm sour smell between them. 'So the Toast of Sanantone is a little upset, eh? Seems to me you've been pawin' dust for quite a while, come to think of it. Tried to give me the slip. Well, the Ranger boy made it, but you didn't.'

'It's been a bad time, Denver. After all, he was my father. And you had Cabbo kill him.'

Mockingly, he lifted his black thicket of eyebrows. 'Why didn't you go live with him, then? In that nester shack. Like he begged you. With that stand-offish kid sister?' His mind whipped to something else. Muttering, he looked vacantly around the room. 'I ought to hold court for her.'

'Why Mary? She's taken an oath. She's no danger to us.'

'More than you think. I'd like to find out. Parker either lied himself too smart or else he scared her off from talking. Everything's fishy. *The goddam Tonks!*' He tore savagely at his hair. 'If I ever get them out of here, I'll fishhook the truth out of her.' He ran his fevered gaze up and down his wife. 'You think I'm crazy,' he said.

Doggedly, she stood her ground. 'Only when you get whiskied up and hold a court. Then—it's inhuman! You and Raffer!'

He looked at her almost blankly, then shook his head a little. 'I hate smart people,' he said again. 'Like this Parker that's come hound-doggin' for something. Like a woman who puts on riding clothes instead of a nightgown.'

Suddenly he stalked around the end of the bed. He stopped before the wide-drawered oak dresser. Her breathing behind him became audible. They both stared down at the tell-tale jumble of white fabric which protruded from a drawer, as if the drawer had been hurriedly closed. Pushing her out of his way, he took three long strides to the edge of the bed, groped under it with a searching boot toe, and kicked out the suitcase. With another foot movement, he kicked back the hinged top and exposed her packed garments.

She had come close behind him. 'It was in case we had to—to run from the Indians—to go to the ranch—'

He threw his massive shoulders back, tilted his huge head and laughed silently. Abruptly the laugh cut off.

'Going somewhere again?' he whispered.

With a grinding oath snarled through clinched bared teeth, he twisted into her shirt front with a mammoth fist, yanked downward in one powerful stroke, and tore the shirt and lace-edged white camisole apart. Buttons flew, clattered on the floor, made tiny rolling noises. She stood mute, head down, full white breasts bared, while he ripped off the rest of the tattered fragments of cloth.

CHAPTER ELEVEN

In the hour before dawn, Mary cautiously worked the key in the lock and swung the door open a crack. Holding her breath against the faint squeaking of hinges, she peeked through and saw the guard asleep in a chair. His head sagged to his chest, his rifle lay on the floor beside the chair, and his snores were louder than the hinges.

In another minute, she was tip-toeing across the long expanse of the first floor, out the entrance, and into the street. She broke into a full run for Rigsby's house.

She burst in upon a room filled with sleepy-eyed nesters, already finishing a skimpy breakfast in the lamplight.

'The judge!' she blurted. 'He's trying to keep me a prisoner!' Anger engulfed her then, as she sensed the fear that shackled these people, their sheeplike resignation to helplessness. Her small hands tightened into fists, and then she saw Mrs. Lige Drain coming toward her.

'Land alive, child! Where have you been? You didn't even come to your pa's buryin'.'

A circle of sympathetic faces closed in around Mary. Mrs. Drain began a voluble flow of condolences, Mary cut her short with an impatient gesture.

'I don't want your talk!' she flared at everybody. 'Where's your backbone? Which one of you wants to be next out there in Boothill with Gus Jenkins? We're rid of Cabbo and Eckhart—but Raffer is still alive! And the judge, and all the others! When are you going to have the guts to do something?'

A sun-peeled little man tried to speak soothingly. 'Now, you're just a mite upset, child. You need a—'

'And you, Glid Clark, you're just a mite cowed and spineless! All of you, just like the Jenkinses—barely existing on your little nester spreads just by sufferance of the Big Man, almost in sight of all the grass in the world. Grass that he hoards—and won't let you touch it! A bunch of—of—' Sputtering, she worked her impassionate gaze from one downcast face to the other. 'A bunch of prairie dogs in a hole, afraid to breathe because the coyote pack is waiting!'

Clark took a mild defensive. 'I'd say the judge's army and the Comanches ain't exactly a little coyote pack, Mary. What chance we got to move in on that grass to the west with all those guns in our back?'

'You're just upset.' Mrs. Drain tried to be consoling again. But for a rare once, her husband publicly differed with her.

'Mary's right,' Drain said hoarsely. 'I'm sick of it. I'm stinkin' sick of it and I hate myself in my sleep.'

Rigsby mopped at a fresh outbreak of sweat. 'You ought to be glad you don't live right here in the settlement, like I do. Where he can get drunk and lock you in that torture chamber of a saloon he's got and put Raffer and his boys to workin' on you. Just for his *enjoyment.* Just for his damn enjoyment, I tell you!'

'Watch your language, Rigs,' his wife said primly.

'To hell with my language!' Rigsby was going full overboard. 'I've heard from Kamack how it happened. That copperhead Cabbo shot her pa square in the back!'

'In the back, mind you!' Drain exploded. 'With him at a window, watching the redskins, doing his part to try to keep them off the settlement if they were a mind to charge us. Like Kamack says, it wasn't Cabbo, that murdered Gus Jenkins. It was *us!*'

Another man nodded reluctant agreement. 'The others just stood, way I heard it. Scared to move. Some stranger had to go after Cabbo and even the score.'

Shrewdly, her wits racing now, her veins red-hot from a fever of vindictive purpose strange to her, Mary Hinton watched them, calculating the slow turnings of their minds.

'You must have had something,' she said evenly, 'just to be out here. Life would have been easier for you east of the Brazos. This simply can't be what you chose to do, to push out from civilization only to run into one big

160

crazy man and turn into slaves!'

'Young woman,' a nester wife complained unhappily, 'you're just tryin' to stir up trouble!'

Mary whirled upon her. 'I'll tell you like a *man*, Mrs. Clark. You damned right I'm trying to stir up trouble! Gus Jenkins was a good man, but my mother was a bad woman—a saloon singer, if you want to know—and there's some of both in me and the bad is breaking out. I *hope* I shock you! I'll tell you to your face like a man you're a bunch of rabbit-twisting nesters, cowards clear down to your fingernails. *Somebody* needs to talk like a man—because there's not a man in all you homesteaders lumped together!'

In their hurt faces she saw the end of her strength to push them further. In another second her emotions would overwhelm her ability to maintain her first hot drunkenness of hate and she would go to pieces, like a little girl, and be shaking on somebody's shoulder with the pent-up sobs that wanted to gush out.

In that tottering moment, when the room, the silent people, blurred crazily, the footstep and voice at the doorway were like a reinforcement coming in time to shoulder a weight that overwhelmed her. She saw his taut expression soften at sight of her. 'Trav!' she breathed.

'She's told you the God's truth,' Trav Parker said quietly. 'You don't look to me like people who'll stomach this Cabbo business forever. I've overheard the talk she handed to you just now. I'll bet you've been telling yourself the same thing, only it had to be this girl that said it out loud for you.' He came on into the room. 'Well, are you going to stand around all your lives holding what she handed you, or do you mean to do something with it?'

'No business of yours, stranger,' one of the men growled.

'Oh, but it is!' Mary said quickly. The fine points of absolute truth went flying from her conscience and she didn't care. 'He's here because it is his business! Don't you even *know*?'

'Know what?' Rigsby frowned.

'He's a Texas Ranger!' Mary almost shouted, hysterically triumphant. 'He's Travis Parker of the Rangers and we've got help now.' Glibly, aware that she might be beginning to break under this unaccustomed role she had thrust herself into, Mary added a flood of sly fabrications: 'A whole battalion of Rangers are coming! He's here to break up the *comanchero* crowd. He's Captain Trav Parker, I tell you! The other Ranger, that was Rotan, and he killed Cabbo.'

Trav shot her a shocked look, then closed his mouth and said nothing. Where was the timid nester girl who washed dishes in the Hinton shack that day? But it didn't matter. She was free, somehow, free from Raffer and

Denver Smith and that was all he needed to gladden his heart.

'Who'll start organizing the homesteaders now?' he demanded. 'You, Drain?'

'Not him!' Mrs. Drain said piteously.

'Shut up!' Drain snorted. 'I'm thinkin'!'

'Think what *he* said out there.' Rigsby pointed a finger at the gauntly intelligent features of Sliff Cage who nonchalantly stood with his tall shoulders against a wall, halfmockingly smiling at the argument.

All the eyes followed Rigsby's forefinger. 'Me?' Cage murmured. He furrowed his high forehead. 'What was that, Rigs?'

Rigsby quoted. 'At Jenkins' funeral. "Therefore we shall not fear, though the earth be moved and though the hills be carried into the sea. There is a river, the streams whereof make glad the city of God, the holy place of the tabernacle of the Most Highest". That's what you said.'

'You have a good memory,' Cage said drily.

'The river the Bible meant might have been the Brazos,' Rigsby told them. 'The tabernacle—maybe it's our job to get it built some day where the Brazos Palace stands.'

Trav nodded. 'I heard the same Bible words said over Shamrock Parker. The meanest drunk in our company said them because he was the only one who knew them. Shamrock Parker was my father. Five minutes after he said them we were firing from behind the

163

rocks again because the Comanches had ringed us for a new attack and they were coming at what was left of us.'

'Shamrock Parker,' Cage said thoughtfully. 'Then that would have been the battle at Concho. Your drunk friend said his buryin' words more times than once that day.'

Trav shook his head. 'Just once. But over seventeen men at the same time. I was barely big enough to be there, but I still hear his words, and I can still see the one grave with all the bodies and the arrow shaft the way it stuck out of Shamrock Parker's throat. After that, all I heard in my sleep for months was the way the Comanches yelled when they came at us again.'

The breeze-rocked door drifted wide open. Trav heard a muttered exclamation from somebody in the room. All heads turned to the doorway to follow this man's frozen line of vision. Trav saw the fluttering spot of color halfway down the road toward the Palace, color that materialized into the running form of a woman. In the same moment all saw the two men running in pursuit.

Mary whispered, 'Wilda!'

Wilda came on, clumsily fighting the sandy road that seized at her ankles, and they saw that she would never make it.

A nester spoke awedly. 'Judge's wife, ain't it? They're gonna grab her 'fore she gets here!'

164

The group crowded to the doorway. They mumbled in sympathetic unison when they saw Wilda stumble and fall. The two men in pursuit closed the distance as she struggled to rise.

A bundle of small muscles exploded through the clustered spectators and shot from Rigsby's cabin.

From where he watched with momentary indecision, peering over the heads of those crowded at the door, Trav yelled, 'Mary! Come back!'

'You can't help her now!' a woman called urgently. 'Come back!'

Recklessly disregarding the chorus of warning behind her, Mary flew toward Wilda. She could do nothing to help the trapped wife of the judge; that was apparent to them all. Yet the small racing figure did not turn back or even slow in response to the imperative calls behind her. Trav began a blind push against the crowd. They gave way before him, all but the last man just outside the door. This one whirled just as Trav cleared the tightly-pressed knot of men and women.

'No you don't!'

Rigsby's fist worked down and up. A sixgun muzzle jabbed squarely into Trav's stomach, stopping him cold.

'Stay where you are, Parker!'

Rigsby pushed hard with the gun muzzle, forcing Trav backward. The nesters gave way.

Rigsby backed him into the room. Beyond Rigsby, Trav got his last sight of Mary stooping over Wilda, as if to assist her to her feet, just as the two pursuing men lumbered upon them. Then somebody kicked the door closed.

Trav tried to make a stand. Rigsby kept prodding him back with the gun in his stomach.

'Goddam you, Rigsby!'

'Easy now, Parker.'

'You let two women get—'

'You couldn't have helped,' Rigsby retorted. 'You'd have got us all in bad trouble.'

'Trouble, hell! I could have made a fight out of it!'

'Wouldn't been much of one. One of those two men was Raffer.'

'So you let Mary fall right into their hands.' Trav shot his bitter accusation at all of them.

'Mary just lost her head,' Rigsby said. 'We got other people to think about, Parker. All of us in this house.'

Drain came forward. 'Rigs is right, Parker. We're on thin ice here, as it is. You don't help any.'

He got a glimmer of their meaning then. Rigsby stepped back, lowering his gun a trifle. 'You see, Parker, it was bad enough for us for Wilda Smith to take off for this house, assumin' that she was runnin' away from the judge. Bad enough for Mary to run out of here, too. Now if you had busted out of my

166

house, on top of all that, we'd have had Raffer and his pack on us in full force. Maybe I could talk my way out of it to the judge on why his wife heads for a bunch of nesters. But I'd never in my life be able to explain what the hell you was doin' here.'

A rumble of agreement went around the room. Heads nodded. Trav shrugged his agreement. He understood, at least a little, how his presence here might endanger the whole lot of them. Yet, out there in the gray morning, Raffer was now marching the two women back to the judge, and his own helplessness sickened him.

In blind disgust he turned away from them and moved toward the back door. As if understanding his feelings, Rigsby said sympathetically: 'There may be other ways we can do something, Parker.'

'Then let me know when you find your guts!' Trav snarled. 'You can get word to me at the Tonkawa camp.' At the door, he had his final word of contempt for them. 'Not that I expect such a miracle to happen!'

He dodged across the open space behind Rigsby's house. The dwelling cut off sight of him from the distant Palace and store building. He jogged toward his horse. In the saddle, riding north out of the settlement, he began to cool off a little. Mary had been foolish, impulsive. What would make her do such a futile thing as run to Wilda's aid? Rigsby and the nester families had a point in not wanting Raffer and his crew to know that they harbored under their roof the stranger who had broken out of the judge's jail. Yet there was gall to taste on his long, circling ride back to the Tonk camp. He had, in a sense, deserted Mary. Twice, now, he had been a party to her capture by the judge's smirking little lawman.

As he approached the Tonk's grove he saw dimly, then plainly in his mind, the tie that would hold him irrevocably to this country. That tie was Mary Hinton. While she lived, he would never be able to ride away alone.

CHAPTER TWELVE

Fire Feather made three finger-tip gullies in the dust.

'Three arroyos west?' Trav flashed three hand chops, nodding. 'How many hands of sun?'

Fire Feather opened his palm four times. Trav went to the coals and brought back a battered can of steaming tea. They squatted and shared it between them. Fire Feather and his scouting party of four had done a good job, Trav told him. Now their white brother was rested. His leg wound felt good. A night of sleep had restored his strength. With the news that Fire Feather had brought, he felt it was time to ride for a look at the judge's ranch headquarters.

The Tonkawa scouts had come back with the news that the rock fort was deserted. Blue Knife's warlike maneuvers had held Smith's cattle crew in the settlement. Trav had been forced to play it adroitly, restraining Blue Knife with tedious trade palaver and at the same time delaying any real agreement. He was using the Tonks as his own cocked gun pointed at the heart of the Smith forces.

Fire Feather had one other item of news. It was bad. The Tonkawa scouts had sighted another burned nester cabin. Comanches!

Fire Feather surreptitiously touched Trav's foot with a patched moccasin. Trav moved a little for easier reach to the Colt on his leg and switched the tea can to his left hand.

Fox One-Eye approached with a rifle dangling at the end of his white-circled arm, and a feather-bedecked tomahawk thrust through the rawhide string that held up his ragged white man's pants.

His guttural speech was too thick for Trav. He looked to Fire Feather. Feather waited, thinking it over in his own way. When Feather was ready, he said, 'Whiskey gone. Say, you go, bring more.' Fox jabbered again. Feather added, 'He not trust any white man. Say you not brother.'

'Has Fox One-Eye taken over the leadership from our great chief, Blue Knife?'

Fox could understand English. He made a deliberate little kick in the dust and the wind sent the flurry of red particles flying into Trav's face.

'Bring whiskey. Bring back white girl,' Fox said distinctly. 'Then you friend of Tonkawas.'

Trav stood up. Fire Feather arose with him, moving aside. A few curious bucks edged near and watched. Fox fingered the head of his tomahawk.

Trav pretended ignorance. 'Bring white girl? Why?'

'You trade her me,' Fox tapped his tattooed chest. 'For Bee-lah.'

'Bee-lah not here.'

Fox jerked a cagey nod, as if that was the whole point he had triumphantly thought out. 'We trade. Bee-lah, white man. Fox, white girl.'

The one-eyed bastard had a longer memory than Blue Knife, Trav thought bleakly. 'How many ponies you pay for white girl?'

Fox gripped his rifle in his left hand. He raised his right, uncovering the head of his tomahawk, to make the signs that helped spoken words. As he did this, beginning a play of hand motions, Trav lunged for the tomahawk at his waist.

Like ripping a part of Fox's body from its socket, he whipped the tomahawk free. As Fox instinctively sprang backward, Trav circled his arm twice and sent Fox's tomahawk spinning to the darkening sky. Every head, including

170

Fox's, snapped back to follow the tomahawk in its flight. In the instant its spent turnings changed and it began the fall to earth, the Colt in Trav's fist bucked and the blast of the .45 rocked the grove.

The tomahawk flew apart like a frog splash in placid water, and pieces of it spewed in all mid-air directions. Trav shoved in a cartridge replacement. That ought to keep harmony for a while longer, he told himself. He waited for the minds of the bucks crowded around to adjust the mental image of what they had seen.

Howls of primitive glee swelled out from the watching warriors. Fox One-Eye pushed through them and plodded in hang-dog fashion out of sight.

Trav holstered the black Colt. Not one damn thing that the trouble-minded Fox could answer with, at least not for the present. The dead white man come-alive who had rejected Bee-lah, had now cost Fox something more than just his pride. The warriors grinned through their paint. Their enjoyment mounted in this ancient symbolism, filthily rowdy in its implication.

A Tonk man had had, his tomahawk go to pieces on him, a misfortune that ofrered crude and fanciful comparisons for the Indian mind in this tribal comedy inherited from their primitive fathers. Mirth overwhelmed the tattooed bucks. If the chunky squaws had been present, they would have started a *milote*, would have mocked Fox by tauntingly parting their cover and shrilling obscene derision for his failing manhood.

The chagrined victim was entitled to do nothing more about it, to his tormentors. than a squaw could do when ridiculed by the men for dropping and cracking a clay cooking pot. It was a thing a warrior should not let happen to him. The tomahawk was a part of his body and it was his lookout to keep it serviceable. If it broke before witnesses, he had no course but to take the jeering torment and remove his disgraced presence for a little while until the convulsed people recovered from their fun in portraying him as a man with an obscene disfigurement. The spectacular circumstance that Fox One-Eye's dismemberment had taken place in mid-air from one magical shot by the white man's loud gun, only added to savage imagination and appreciation.

Trav faded from among them, into the trees. This was a good time for him to vanish. He lifted his saddle to the mustang, rode south a way in case either red or white man could see the dark dot of him in the twilight, and then swung back west and north. Three deep arroyos to cross in the plains beyond, Fire Feather had said. Three deep arroyos somewhere west, distance like four hands of sun, to the judge's ranch house. The scar in his rib skin pulled a little, as it always did in a slow lope, to renew its reminder that he lived only to find the man who had put it there.

*   *   *

The place, when he sighted it, rose up
unexpectedly in the solitude. Although these
vast stretches of plain appeared level, viewed
from far-off, the land concealed in its own
shadows of distance a series of rises and
troughs, with an occasional deeper arroyo
where the gurgle of cold springs sounded.
Somewhere south, these sinks would begin to
bunch upon themselves like sea breakers.
Then the earth as far as any eye could see
reared up in an east-west line of jagged, rocky
folds resembling stormy ocean waves frozen
solid at the peak of their dark curling plunge.
This was the mysterious Fault Scarp, the Texas
Cap Rock that Trav had crossed at its eastern
beginning some days back when he and Rotan
first scouted this side of the Brazos.

And it was in such a stretch of shallow cuts
that he looked first upon the mesquite flat and
saw the houses. There were two of them, one
squat and square, the other some distance
removed with the narrow shape of it backed up
against the outlines of a sizable corral.

Trav reined into cover and tied the
mustang. He made a careful approach and lay
flat for a long time behind a rock outcropping.
After this, he brought the horse up to the same
place, staked it again where it could not be

173

skylighted, and continued afoot. At the edge of a weedy open space, he jogged to the nearest shadowed corner of the corral. From here he worked his way along the narrow building, around its end, and to a doorway. He listened a long time, hearing no sound not rightfully made by the night, then tried the door latch.

The structure, which he took to be a bunkhouse, was locked tight. A wood-shuttered window near the doorway also proved to be fastened inside. He dug into the crack of the wood frame with his knife. He whittled space enough to make a crevice that would take the muzzle of his gun, and pried hard with this. Something gave, and the solid plank shutter drifted open.

Now he could see inside. As his eyes worked at it, he began to fathom the outlines of bare bunks along the walls. He smelled the sweaty and leathery paraphernalia of any bunkhouse or barracks. He moved on to the pole corral, found it empty. Then he headed for the dark shape that he took for the judge's rock fort.

The place was a fort, all right. The few windows were shoulder high, narrow, and shuttered with thick timber. The two doors were heavier timber, bolted through massive iron hinges. The judge had taken no chances when he set up his trading point for Comanche dealings. If he and his crew ever got behind those stone walls, in case of trouble, the

Comanches would have a hard time driving them out. Just a few men with rifles to cover the good furlong of open ground any attacking redskins would have to cross, could hold off repeated charges.

Trav fingered over the door slab in the dark, examining by touch the thick iron chain and massive padlock. It seemed as if he had ridden all the dim trails just to get to this doorway. Unless the judge kept his personal effects in the Brazos Palace, something of the man's past ought to lie beyond this door. Some little clue, some telltale item that a Ranger could read well enough to help piece together the story of Denver Smith. He pressed against the stone wall, out of reach of flying metal, unless it showered his hand, and put a .45 slug into the lock.

He listened relaxed for five full minutes, trying to keep every muscle slack to free his cars from inner crackling. The Colt's boom played out. The night stayed silent.

He returned to the trees on the slope. He rode the mustang back to the yard, took off saddle and bridle, and staked the mount in the weeds where a yard-wide spring bubbled downgrade through a gravel ditch.

Inside, he found the iron bar that secured the door, and then held his sixgun ready while he struck a match on the stone wall. Its flutter of flame showed shadowed pieces of furniture and kitchen gear at the end of the room. An open doorway led to the other room. This proved to be a bedroom. The personal effects he sighted by match light indicated it was the judge's and Wilda's private quarters.

He sat on the edge of the bed in the darkness, running a hand over the woolly fuzz of a blanket, and into the cotton coolness of sheets underneath. Four or five hours left, he estimated, till dawn. He pried off his boots, removed his outer clothes, and slid between the sheets with his sixgun under the pillow. Sleepily, dead-tired, he fixed his wake-up intention for the first stir of prairie hens at gray dawn. Then it would be up to daylight to show him whatever it might have to reveal here. He went to sleep at once.

*   *   *

Raffer reported at mid-morning.

'Some Indians driving the wagon back, judge. They're stopped about halfway out there, like they want somebody to come get it.'

'How many Indians?'

'Two. One on the wagon, the other horseback, leading a mount for the wagon driver. Wing says they make signals they got a message.'

The judge headed out to the road where he could see the open country south. The wagon and a mounted Tonkawa were visible but far off. 'They want that wagon filled up again,' the

176

judge muttered. He thought a moment. 'Take Wing and ride out there. See what they want and bring the wagon back.' Raffer rode off to find Wing, the half-breed. A little later, they trotted their horses toward the wagon. Raffer and Wing pulled up within speaking distance. The Indian on the wagon climbed down, warily watching, and mounted the spare pony the other Indian was leading. The one-eyed buck made hand signs. Wing answered.

'They want the wagon loaded up again,' Raffer said, reading the signs. 'What're they after this time?'

'Guns. Whiskey.'

'Tell 'em anything. Tell 'em all right. You drive the wagon in.'

Wing spoke in Tonkawa. One of the Indians appeared satisfied. He turned his pony and started back for the Tonkawa camp. The other, the one-eyed one, lingered. He looked at Raffer with his good eye and motioned with the rifle. He grunted a few words in Tonkawa.

'Speak English!' Raffer commanded. 'All Tonks know some English. What you want?'

'Me Fox One-Eye,' the Indian said, flourishing his rifle. 'Tobacco.' He spieled off a flow of Tonkawa.

Wing said from the wagon seat, 'He wants to trade some news for your sack of tobacco. He's scared of what he's doing, but he's fired up. Be careful.'

Raffer pulled a tobacco sack and tossed it

across. One-Eye caught it with his free hand. Then, speaking in Tonkawa, English, and hard sign, he told Raffer that the white man had ridden west. Somewhere to the white chief's ranch house. White man looking for something.

Raffer listened carefully. 'Parker? You mean Tonk white friend, name of Parker?'

Fox One-Eye nodded. 'Parker.'

Raffer thought this over. 'Dammit, Wing, it was worth a sack of tobacco.'

Wing made a mistake, then. He said something to Raffer in the Comanche dialect. Comanche words coming unexpectedly from the hair-braided breed on the wagon seat must have unsettled the Tonkawa, or else Fox One-Eye was in a high state of nervousness over his act of treachery. As if the Comanche had physically threatened him, Fox turned his rifle in a quick defensive motion. Its muzzle pointed at Wing. Raffer's hand flashed. His revolver blasted, and a red spot festered out between Fox's good eye and the empty one. Fox pitched from his mustang with rifle unfired and the pony bucked and ran. Raffer got down and put another bullet into the tattooed body. He retrieved his sack of tobacco, picked up Fox's rifle, and looked for the buck's tomahawk to lift as a trophy. The Indian's rawhide belt was empty, however, so Raffer legged into his saddle and motioned for Wing to come on with the wagon. He hit a lope for the settlement with some news he thought would interest the judge.

*   *   *

The day worried along cool and overcast, but at high noon the sun went out of sight completely and low black thunderclouds rolled in. The land darkened. Trav had found nothing in Denver Smith's personal effects to offer light on the man's past. He worked now in the bunkhouse, trying at the same time to watch the country, which meant going to the windows every little while. Yet there were so many rises and gullies in the distant gloom that he doubted if his vigilance was worth-while. He began to have the feeling of walking on soft ice.

Trouble, when it came, showed up with no more sound than a copperhead oozing out of a hole. They must have made their approach from the west, with the rock building between them and the bunkhouse where he had painstakingly examined each item of every man's possessions. He walked from the bunkhouse into the cloud-darkened open and into a nest of gun muzzles.

There were six of them.

'Turn your back,' Raffer said.

'Now take it easy, Raffer.' He saw from the way the marshal's eyes glazed over that he was not going to outtalk Raffer in this. He turned,

179

but he was too slow to suit Raffer. The bullet slammed out and proved Raffer's deadliness with that Colt. The slug accurately sliced the upper sleeve of Trav's jacket. He felt the burn nip across his skin.

'Now drop your gun on the ground,' Raffer said. 'Go pick it up, Guerra.'

At his back, Guerra muttered, 'You choked me that night at the jail. Remember?' From the tail of his eye, Trav saw the raised boot and the sharp rowel. The spur slashed across the back of his leg. The steel rowel points bit in, stabbing into the spot of his barely healed leg wound. Trav staggered from pain and went dizzy. Guerra slapped him hard at the back of his neck with his sixgun and Trav went down fighting the sudden darkness.

When he came to, he found that they had lugged him into the judge's house. Somebody had bandaged his leg. He sat upon the floor. They looked indifferently at him and went on with their meal.

'We tied up your leg,' Raffer said. 'Couldn't let you bleed to death on us.'

When they were ready to ride, Raffer said, 'Tie his hands behind him, somebody. Then get him on his horse.'

Trav said, 'No need for that. There're six of you. That would be Apache business.' He knew the torture that came to a man riding with wrists bound behind him.

Raffer wet his lips. 'Tie him up, Guerra.

He's a foxy one.'

Guerra stalked forward with a short length of rope.

'Forgot to tell you, Parker,' Raffer murmured. 'You're under arrest.'

CHAPTER THIRTEEN

They cut the rope in front of the Brazos Palace in the twilight and he sat for a time without moving, blind to the bustle around him, unable to take his hands from behind his back. Raffer called, 'Get down.'

Trav muttered, 'I'm going to kill you for this, Raffer.'

'They always say that.'

One of the men went inside and shortly came back. 'He says bring him in.'

'Pull him off his horse,' Raffer ordered.

A man did this and Trav found himself sprawled in the dust. Pain seized him all over and his bad leg buckled twice before he could stay on his feet.

Someone locked the door behind them. Trav sighted the judge leaning against the bar midway down, facing a collection of hardcase watchers assembled like an audience. The hanging lamps gave his features a yellowed gauntness. He had a blue lupine twig, its petals drooping, in his lapel, and a whiskey bottle and a law book on the table drawn up in front of him.

Without removing his elbows that hooked him to the bar, he hung a glassy black stare on Trav as if he had never seen him before.

'So you had to take a little trip.'

Trav rubbed his circulation back into action. 'Call off your pack, Smith. We can talk this over between ourselves.'

As if he needed to establish his jurisdiction, Smith intoned, 'This is court. I'm the judge of all the land north of the Brazos.'

'You're a damn fool!' Trav retorted. 'This kangaroo court business is crazy . . .' He trailed off his last words, feeling he was talking to a body with its brain left somewhere else.

The brain worked, however. 'What's become of your partner?'

'He's at the Tonk camp.'

'What were you looking for at my place?'

The man had him and no lie came to mind that would help. Each knew who the other was and Smith had only one way to deal with this ghost from his old and haunting crime. In this pause, Raffer suggested, 'Let's convene court, judge.'

'Court's convened,' Smith said.

Trav said, 'Judge, either you like to play a Roman emperor here or you're crazy from whiskey. Some friends of mine below the Brazos are not going to like this. Why don't we call it off and talk a little sense to each other?'

Smith unhooked himself from the bar and took a drink. 'What's the charge, Mr. Marshal?'

'Burglarizin' the ranch house, Your Honor. Resisting legal arrest. Murder of Eckhart and Cabbo. Breakin' jail. We got all kinds of charges.'

'What does the defendant say?'

Trav prodded his mind for just any faint means to deal with this, but nothing offered a way out. He bleakly visioned his situation being like that of an Apache captive staked naked on an anthill. He returned Smith's stare. 'Did that ambush addle your brain, judge?'

A visible shaking started in Smith's hands, working up his arms, contorting his facial flesh. Raffer said hurriedly, 'Defendant don't talk, judge. You want Ike to start with the bullwhip?'

While the judge rattled the neck of a whiskey bottle against a glass, a chunky man with silky red beard got up, holding a coiled black bullwhip in his hand. He sauntered toward the door, taking a stance in the open, and trained his sight at Trav's arm. Trav turned his numbed attention on the embalmed features of the marshal. All the hate in him came to a focus on Raffer. Raffer hadn't needed to tie his hands behind him for that torturous gallop back. All he asked now, was to live long enough to kill Raffer.

So when the judge blinked at the bullwhip

man to give them a show, Trav barely flinched. Red Beard's arm worked carefully. The bite of the streaking leather curled snakily out for an exploratory nip. Trav sat rigid, watching Raffer, so he would not jerk and throw off the whip marksman's aim and maybe lose an eye. The rest of the strained faces showed as yellow blurs. From the corner of his eye, Trav measured the distance to the whip man. The whip wrap itself would yank him halfway. He collected his leg muscles.

When the next whip crack wrapped the weighted end snapper around his dangling wrist, with Red Beard fishing him up from the chair, Trav churned his legs under him and kept plowing all the way across the floor upon the assured performer. The chunky one might have expected to snake the tall stranger forward a few feet. But when Trav kept coming in a rush, confusion showed on Red Beard. He tried to switch the whip butt to his left hand. Too late, he stumbled backward from the impact, exposing his holstered gun. Trav had him. With a side twist, he pulled the man's Colt, encircled his neck with his left arm, and wrenched the chunky one in front of him. Now he had a gun and a living shield.

Trav tightened his arm on the throat and held the sixgun on the room, pressing it against the squirming whip man's side. But he saw that Raffer was going to shoot regardless, even if the bullet got the wrong man. The struggling one choked out a frenzied, 'No! No!' Raffer took aim. Trav tightened his finger on the trigger, making the light squeeze action come off sure on Raffer's narrow chest. The man he held jumped off the floor from the bite of the powder burn against his bottom rib, and the muzzle's fire streak seemed to reach on and on, poking Raffer into a prancing fall.

There were more guns on Trav than he could look at a thicket of black muzzle holes. The weight of the panicked, gagging man who clawed at the locked arm across his gullet unbalanced them both and they fell in a tangle. The revolver flew out of his hand. When he rolled clear, he had no time to lunge for his own holstered Colt that someone had left on a table near the door.

The judge walked between Trav and the gumnen. 'Don't kill him. He won't do me any good till I know what might be coming behind him.'

'Those coming behind me carry a tight noose, Denver.'

Somebody said, 'Raffer's a goner, judge.'

Smith flung off a finger of sweat. 'What's the matter with you, Ike?' Red Beard muttered a defense. Smith looked meaningfully at his men. 'She doesn't like gunfire in here.'

He took a drink and turned back. 'All right. Three or four of you hold him with his arm across a table.' He drew his Colt and grasped it by the barrel. 'We'll start by relieving him of that trigger finger.'

Four men got up and cautiously moved upon Trav. They were stopped by the dramatically low voice that came from the back gloom of the stairway.

'You'll do no such thing, Denver Smith!'

Wilda walked into the light as if coming upon a stage. A painted red smile outlined her mouth. Her hand gracefully clutched the folds of the loose pink robe draping her body, and as she walked forward the swinging folds parted a little to show white flashes of bare ankles above her redstrapped high-heeled shoes.

Every head turned. Wilda stepped agilely upon the first chair she came to, and from there to a table top, this climb exposing a glimpse of bare knees. She stood on the table, the smile drawn red around small white teeth, her hips swaying a little.

The judge knuckled his mouth. He leaned against the bar, haggard, and muttered weakly, 'Get out of here. Court's in session.'

'Court's over!' Wilda retorted. 'I've got nothing on underneath, Denver.'

He choked. 'You wouldn't do it!'

'I've told you what I'd do.'

'You wouldn't do it!' he repeated thickly.

'And they would all remember,' she said relentlessly. 'Every time you saw one of your men from here on, he would look at you and

186

remember. You're so jealous, honey! Do you think you could kill all of them for what they'd been privileged to look at?'

Smith shuddered. Trav could only stare, like the others, in disbelief for what he saw and heard. The one thing that stood out in this stark duel between Srnith and his wife was Wilda's assurance. They could all see that it was Smith who burned with shame. Certainly none showed on Wilda.

'Get out!' Srnith mumbled.

'Adjourn court, then. It's my way of fighting back, Denver. You know I'll do it. Don't make me.'

Every man craned toward her.

You slut!' the judge said.

Wilda's face reddened and the smile strained to hang on. Her words struck at him like claws. 'But I'm naked underneath and I'll prove it to the whole room if you don't let this man walk out of here, right now!'

'I'll kill you first!' It was a hollow threat.

'Oh, no you won't! I've got it all in writing somewhere, Denver.'

The smoke-heavy air seemed to close down with the moment's indecision. The judge looked at his wife, then at his slack-mouthed jury. Tantalizingly, she rustled the loosely clutched edges of her robe. 'Your jury has never seen a witness like me, Denver.'

Trav saw his chance, the gamble that was better than none, and lifted his gunbelt from the table, turned his back, and walked unhurriedly to the front door. He worked the lock, his spine feeling bared for a bullet, but the silence held as he stepped into the night and closed the door behind him. Then he ran for the nearest horse at the hitch-rack.

He spurred the horse in a scrambling plunge for the back of the building, and strained to see the second-floor windows in the darkness. There was no outside porch on the south wing, and the white movement at the small rear window showed plainly. It was Mary Hinton. He fought the horse to a pawing stop as he shook out the coiled rope from the saddle-horn.

'Stand back a little,' he called to her. 'Catch the loop.'

He threw. The rope's small noose disappeared into the yawning blackness, slacked a moment, then tightened. He dropped the coil at the side of the building and watched Mary's shadowy figure emerge and slide down. He caught her as she came level to the saddle. She slipped behind him and locked her arms about his waist and he drove in the spurs. The animal made a wild dash for the back of the building just as the sounds of running feet came from the front of the Palace. The trance created by Wilda's promising challenge had at last been broken. The judge's crew came tardily after their quarry. The judge's crazed roar of commands drifted into the night.

'Hang on!' Trav gritted. Two small arms tightened convulsively about him. He braced himself in the stirrups, and worked the sixgun out of the belt where he had looped it over the saddle-horn. He kneed the horse until he had a quartering angle toward the darkness behind him. He raised his right arm and squeezed off the bullets, one after another, until the hammer struck with a thin click. The storm of hoof noise rose only from beneath him as the frightened horse leveled for a short run into the night. Trav pulled him down to a head-tossing trot, then to a walk.

'You're a good rider.'

'You're good to hold to,' her lips whispered at his ear.

'Good at sliding down a rope, too. Burn your hands?'

'I don't feel anything. Just numb.'

They were in the dark open country now, headed south, toward the Tonkawa camp. 'You trust me yet?' Trav asked.

The small voice so close behind him was slow in its answer. 'I don't have much choice.'

Later, as he sat across from her in Blue Knife's *tipi*, he gravely explained that good judgment dictated both of them should ride out of the country. Only Wilda's brazen performance had given him this chance to leave. Yet, to himself, he considered the other course. Raffer's appearance at the ranch with

189

his gunmen could be a give-away sign that Smith was afraid to have his place ransacked. If so, the search there had to be completed. He thought back. He hadn't explored the log-adobe shed at the far end of the corral, or those dim wagon tracks running north and out of sight into an arroyo. He glanced up from the fire.

'You want to tell me anything, Mary?' He felt, rather than saw, her small body stiffen in resistance. 'Never mind,' he said hurriedly. 'No time to get into another wrangle. You ready to ride?'

'Anything to get away.'

He went outside and found Blue Knife. In a little while he returned with two horses. Reining alongside him, Mary said, 'What did you say to Blue Knife? What are they going to do?'

'Before long the judge's court will have its hands full.'

'You mean you sent them to attack the village?' She sounded indignant.

He changed their route a little, swinging west. 'Why not? You want the judge's crew chasing us?'

'No—o—o. But an Indian attack. It seems such a bloodthirsty thing to do. To white people.' She put accusation in her tone.

He could have told her it wouldn't be a very bloody attack. Just a surprise action, more wild shots and yelling than anything else. But enough to hold Denver Smith's army in the houses. At least, he hoped that would be the limit of Blue Knife's show. The Tonkawas were getting incensed over the delay in making a trade.

'Too bad about the Tonks being bloodthirsty. When Wilda Smith stopped the proceedings back there the Roman emperor was getting ready to hammer a finger off me.'

The small boyish figure riding alongside seemed to shrink even smaller in the saddle. 'What did she do?'

He told her, bluntly.

'It was something like a stage for her,' Mary murmured. 'An audience. Then she saw in you her chance to get away from Brazos Pass. There was some revenge in it, too. Against Denver.'

'I say she showed wonderful courage.'

Flatly, Mary replied, 'You don't think I've got much. Do you?'

If he could prod her into anger, maybe he could trick some answers out of her. 'I don't see you calling your husband's hand by threatening to strip naked in front of a crowd of men. You won't even expose your thoughts.'

'There's more than one kind of courage,' she retorted. Then, in a small voice, 'I suppose you admire her.'

He wanted to blurt that more than anything he admired the nester girl at his side, that he knew real courage when he saw it. But he would play his cards as he had started. 'You could use some of the same blood in your veins that Wilda's got.'

Her reply, when it finally came, just puzzled him. 'That's an interesting thought, Trav.'

He said roughly, defeated: 'I might as well tell you. We're headed for the judge's place. You can go with me, or you can head back for Brazos Pass, or turn for the river and civilization.'

'Why to the judge's ranch?'

'Because I've got something to do there. Also, it's the last place they'd look for me now. Well, which way do you want to go?'

'I want to stay with you,' she said simply.

He lost all his intentions to badger her into talking against her will. They rode on through the dark folds of the prairie, silent with their thoughts. One thought endured in Trav's mind. He, too, wanted her to stay with him. Now, and from here on.

*　　　*　　　*

The saddle hanging on the fourth peg back stopped him. The morning's first sun streaks came into the log and 'dobe shed through the door at his back and touched the frayed red leather and tarnished silver trim. Then he touched it, too, with a tingling in his fingertips.

The saddle was his.

His mind went back to other years, to the

man who had given it to him.

He lifted the faded, brush-scarred left skirt. The old embossed name had been blotted out. But he found faint traces of it. The crude later tooling of the name DENVER SMITH did not completely conceal the earlier hand-stamped letters that once spelled SHAMROCK PARKER. He recognized the familiar features as if he were seeing long-absent kin, because a man's saddle became a part of him and the little things about it were indelible elements of his daily life. This one had carried three owners, Shamrock Parker, Travis Parker and Denver Smith. It was hard worn, but its individual design and quality had been striking enough that Denver Smith had not been able to discard it.

After a while, he walked along the old wagon tracks, followed them to the cliff base, and sighted the shoulder-high opening of a cave. He stooped and pushed through the dead briar vines. He found himself in a log-braced cavern, larger than a good-sized room.

He retraced his route to the house, burdened with a heavy load in his arms. Mary came to the doorway of the squat stone house and looked for him against the morning sun.

She stepped aside when Trav walked in and followed him to where he placed the heavy wooden crate upon the table at the kitchen end of the first room. When he pried off the wood covering with a poker, they both stared down at the six Henry rifles and a scattering of boxes marked '.44 Caliber Rimfire.'

Mary breathed, 'What does this mean, Trav?'

'There's a cave full of 'em, down there.' He took up one of the rifles, wiped the grease off it, levered the action, and began to load the magazine.

'Denver Smith's latest collection, for his next trade with the Comanches. Rifles and kegs of whiskey.'

Mary looked at him strangely. 'Then, you know.'

Now that he had found the proof he had searched for so long, he felt no elation. Instead, there was the dull wonderment of how to get Denver Smith in sight over the muzzle end of the Colt in his holster.

'My old saddle,' he said quietly. 'It's hanging in the shed.'

'This is what you've been looking for?'

'For over a year. Some tangible evidence, something that would take all the guesswork out of it. I thought the name would be Jack Hinton, when I found the end of the trail. I never heard of Denver Smith until I hit Brazos Pass. Now I know the man who did it, and I know what my next job is.' He put down the loaded Henry and turned to her. 'What I don't know is why you shielded him.'

'I didn't shield him!'

'At least, you've never told me why Jack

Hinton changed his name, why you and your father lived out here under Denver Smith's bare sufferance.'

'I was afraid,' she said.

'Afraid of what?'

'Of you.'

'Why? How do you mean?'

'Because you were a Ranger. We thought you were out to arrest him—my father.'

'Why?'

'For trying to murder you that time.'

'Go ahead.'

'For a long time, my father thought you were dead. Then he heard rumors you were alive.'

'Then he changed his name?'

'He'd already done that. Denver Smith had planted it everywhere that Jack Hinton did the ambush! My father thought he was a fugitive, that he would be shot on sight by the Rangers, because he knew how they would avenge a thing like that. He tried to make Jack Hinton disappear.'

'Couldn't you start at the beginning,' he said gently. 'Tell it straight through?' There must be something more, something she still concealed.

'There's another person—' But her voice died off. Then, forlornly: 'Did it ever occur to you I might have been sworn to a secret?'

He caught sight of far-off movement through the open door. He took up a new rifle and hurried to the yard.

'It's a woman.' he said over his shoulder to Mary, tensed behind him. 'She's bee-lining for this place.'

Mary gripped his arm. Her hand shook a little. 'Wilda!' she whispered. She shaded her eyes against the sunlight. 'She'll be angry.'

'With me?' Trav asked.

'With both of us,' Mary said in awkward innocence. 'She'll think—Wilda will believe something—that's not so—that we couldn't be here together unless—'

Trav could not restrain a grin trace as he looked down at her anxious pinched-cheek face. 'I can hardly believe it, myself,' he murmured.

For the first time, she exposed something in her direct gaze at him that was bold and reckless. She stood with feet spread, tossing her head hoydenishly. He clearly heard her say, 'Neither can I!' and saw this unexpected daring immediately take refuge behind a pinkish little-girl blush for her own shocking audacity. That was when Travis Parker identified the thing that had been fanning the back of his brain like a fledgling's wing. It was very simple. He was in love with the nester's daughter. He had been in love with her ever since the moment she had fired a derringer bullet into his general direction with her head turned childishly the other way. But she was no child. Far from it. She was a woman. They stood together and waited for Wilda Smith to cross the open ground to the rock house.

CHAPTER FOURTEEN

The rock-walled house had heard many *comanchero* trades vehemently argued by vicious men. The scars were there, brown stains that had once been blood. White traders dealt from a muck of contempt heaped upon them by the red; the palefaces were the ones peddling death to be used against their own kind. The red man's viciousness was born of having to come to the outlaw whites for their needs in the first place. Each hated the other. Guns, whiskey and stolen cattle slaked their hostility for a little while, just long enough for these things to be settled in the mutual self-debasement of the trade and of pandering to the requirements of an enemy. After that, the Comanches and Denver Smith's forces parted, each going its way with such benefits as had been gained, and with new hatred and contempt for the ally.

But, for all their evil past, the rock walls of this room had never quite heard the like of the tirade loosened by the spiteful tongue of this robust woman scorned.

Before her agitation played out, Wilda's hair had shaken loose, her cheek powder went

197

criss-crossed with tear tracks, and finally she simply looked old, spent, helpless. She flung herself into a chair and covered her face.

'That was a brave thing you did for me,' Trav said quietly.

'What did it get me?' her muffled voice replied.

Mary said, 'It got you what you started out to make yourself deserve, Wilda. Nothing but sorrow at the end.'

Wilda took her hands down to fling a scorching glare at the younger girl. 'Miss Innocence!' she rasped. 'Freckled-faced little sister! You ran off with him! You had to—'

'Wilda!'

'I suppose you've spilled it all out to him. All about your bad sister! The ambush—!'

'Please, Wilda!' Mary cast a horrified glance at Trav. 'Don't say anything more!'

'And what else has my pious little sister done with the big Ranger besides talk!'

Trav came unlocked from where he sat with a leg hooked over the table and put down the greasy new rifle he had been loading. Rigidly, with his blood pumping loud in his ears, he stalked heavy-legged across to Wilda. Even Mary's small, woeful cry of protest was lost to the surge of heat in his veins, the hammering knowledge of discovery.

'Did you say sister?'

Wilda stabbed a long finger at Mary. 'I knew she would tell it all some day! The ambush, everything!'

Trav's fingers locked on Wilda's wrist. He pulled her erect, purposeful in his roughness. 'The ambush! The third man that night, with Denver Smith. You, Wilda?'

She nodded dumbly.

He whirled to Mary. Her expression was the give-away. He shook Wilda's arm viciously. 'The skeleton up there!' he said. 'The bones in the Territory. The man Denver killed. Was it because of you?'

Wilda weakly whispered the name.

'Gus Jenkins.'

She pulled away from Trav and fell into the chair again, eyeing him vacantly as if nothing mattered now. 'Denver caught on. He got jealous of Gus and killed him after they robbed you.'

'And you were the one who rode off toward Texas. The one the Tonkawas thought was a man.'

'I didn't want to see it. Gus was supposed to have killed Denver afterwards, like we'd planned. We were going on together, Gus and the money and me, down to Texas. But Denver was smarter.'

'In the argument in your camp, before the ambush, the Tonkawas heard the name 'Jack Hinton' called. Do you remember that?'

Wilda nodded blankly. 'One of them might have yelled out something about my father. Gus and Denver were very mad at each other.

My father refused to join Denver in the ambush plan. He left us at Abilene, and Denver got Gus Jenkins to ride with us. I might as well tell you—I was the one who planned it all in the first place. I saw how Denver and I could be rich. Gus was a handsome man from Montana, or somewhere. We met up with him at Abilene. When we found out that you'd come north to get the herd money, I talked them into waylaying you on the ride back.'

Mary came over and touched Trav's arm. 'These are things I was sworn never to tell,' she said softly. 'When my father came back, he knew Denver had put it out that Jack Hinton had killed you. He was afraid of the Rangers. As I told you, Trav, my father thought that Jack Hinton had to disappear off the earth. Denver got him to take the name of Gus Jenkins. He let us live here, so he could keep an eye on us, I guess. And my father wanted to be near Wilda. He always felt that he was to blame, somehow, for what she had—turned out to be. He was afraid of arrest, afraid to leave this country. I guess he was just trying to bear a part of Wilda's guilt in that awful thing by staying somewhere close to her, and suffering his life out.' She peered at her sister. 'You. know that, don't you, Wilda? You knew how he felt about you?'

Trav turned away from them, seeing it now, reconstructing the Abilene plot and the

200

Territory robbery, the money-crazed woman planning it, her affair with the handsome stranger from Montana, the argument on the trail, and Denver Smith's way of taking care of Gus Jenkins who had looked too greedily upon Denver's wife and the chance of easy money.

When he glanced back again, he saw that Mary had placed a consoling hand upon Wilda's bent shoulder. Wilda's body shook with muffled crying. He heard Mary say, 'I tried to keep my word.'

Wilda moved her hand to seize Mary's and held on to it. 'I know!' she said tearfully. 'I know! You were better, stronger than all of us. I guess I always knew that in my heart.'

'How did you get away from Brazos Pass?' Trav asked.

'The Tonkawas—they started an attack. In all the excitement I found a horse and just struck out. I knew you'd come here before. I gambled that you'd come here again.'

Trav stepped to the open doorway. In a little while the sun would be down. Getting the two of them out of the country was his job now. He would take them on a circuituous swing south of Brazos Pass, and then they would strike for the river trails. His search, he supposed, had to be considered finished. Maybe he could make his story convincing to Captain Small. He'd just have to forget about getting Denver Smith in his gunsight. The vital problem was to escort the two women to safety, to save their lives and his own, for the judge would be desperate to silence all three.

Off a distance in the first mesquites, a pair of scissortails flew in, still darting angrily about over some recent peeve. The late breeze rippled a flowing shadow play across the grass and low brush of the northern breaks. He caught the far-away blur of a coyote in a high run, chasing nothing visible. He stiffened.

He smelled closely of his hands, from which he had wiped the gun grease, and sniffed against the gentle breeze. He disengaged his shoulder from the timbered doorway. He reached back to lift the rifle and sauntered on without attracting the attention of the two women who sat close together, talking in undertones.

Beyond the corral he kept to the low slope, crossed the rocky arroyo, limped up the other side and stopped just before the rim skylighted him. Here he went to his stomach and crawled upward until he could observe over the broomweeds and midget cedars at the crest. He studied the shadowed ridges to the north. He watched until the sun went down. Closer than before, he spotted the dark running shape of another coyote floating across the skyline, not circling as in a rabbit chase. Trav inhaled deeply, trying to sort the elements of breeze odors, to tell one from the other or what was imagination and what wasn't. He back-crawled down the slope, then trotted at a stoop into the canyon bottom and to the cave. Once more he climbed the south edge and followed the wagon tracks to the yard, bent with another crate of rifles and ammunition.

The two women had not lighted a lamp. Wilda sat silent and more composed, now. Mary came toward Trav as he entered, but he pushed past her and began to open the second crate. When she brought over a lamp he shook his head.

'Not yet. I can see all right.'

Mary studied him. 'Why more rifles, Trav?'

Something in Mary's voice caused Wilda to stand. Trav looked them over thoughtfully. How much help would they be?

'I'd like you to close all the window shutters,' he said. 'See that the bolts are in place. One of you put the bar across the door.'

'Comanches!' Mary said.

'It's just to be on the safe side. Can you two handle a Henry?'

Mary said, 'Of course.'

'There's portholes in the shutters,' Wilda said. 'Denver always said a dozen whites could hold off two hundred Comanches in here.'

'We're not a dozen whites.'

He tried to figure their chances. Two women and himself. Twelve rifles. One hundred and eighty rounds ready to be levered and fired, plenty of ammunition for reloads. Four walls to be watched, but they could close off and bar the other room. He walked over to

203

them, and they stood together a moment, three shadows, caught in the silence and their fear.

'Wilda, was a delivery due to be made soon?'

'Those things I never knew about,' she whispered. 'I've overheard, a little. All the men usually come here and fort up in case of trouble. Denver never trusted the—those people he dealt with. I think only a few came first to this house, a Mexican or a *comanchero* who spoke like a Mexican.'

'Denver usually dealt with this man?'

'I've heard the name Gilo. When the cattle or horses were delivered, and whatever else they had brought to trade, the war party would come and get the rifles and whiskey.'

'Then Denver's crew would drive the cattle off to grass?'

'Yes. There must be thousands of head out there. Ever so often he sells a big herd to the Indian agencies up north.'

They listened through the dragging dark hours, ears first to one window, then another. Time limped on toward midnight and then Mary crept over to touch Trav's arm. 'Come to the north window. I heard something.'

He fixed the sounds, in a little while, over toward the corral. Then he heard a mustang's whinny. From a window cautiously opened on that side, he watched until the two shadows materialized. The riders stopped midway across the yard. They appeared to be waiting.

They would think it strange if there was no hail from the house. He had no way of knowing what Denver's procedure would have been. He would try to bluff it through.

He called out: 'Who is it?'

'Gilo,' a guttural voice answered. 'Gilo and Hawktree. You Smith?'

'I'm acting for Smith. Ride in closer, Gilo.'

The two walked their ponies quite near the window, apparently without alarm. The Mexican voice said, 'We're ready to do business. You Smith man?'

'Where's your main party?'

'Back a ways.'

The girls whispered protests against his going. 'It's got to be done,' he told them. 'If they get the idea something's fishy, they might hit with that whole war party. Bar the door behind me.'

He caught up a lamp, removed the chimney, and carried it and a rifle to the door. He let himself out and walked into the yard. Now he could make out the heavy rider in white man's garb and the feather-tipped Comanche on the other horse. 'Follow me, Gilo. You and Hawktree. I'll show you the trade stuff.' Off-handedly, he added, 'I've got plenty of men here to help load in the morning.'

They walked their horses behind him to the arroyo and the cave opening. He lighted the lamp. Gilo and Hawktree stared hard at him before turning to view the gun crates and whiskey kegs.

'You new man,' Gilo said. Hawktree lingered near the opening. The Comanche was leery. Trav hoped Gilo would take the lead in showing how the trade talk was supposed to go. Instead, Gilo looked hurriedly around at the cache and headed for the opening. Trav extinguished the sputtering wick flame. Outside, Gilo said something in Comanche. Trav missed Gilo's husky pronunciations but he knew the Indian replied, *'No like!'*

Trav switched the rifle to his left arm with the lamp, so that his right hand was free at his gun holster. Gilo walked a few paces through the boulders.

Trav waited tensely as Gilo planned his move, trying to watch both dark figures at once as they waited for him on the path. His worst fears were confirmed when he heard the sound of scraping on leather. He could not distinguish it in the dark, but he knew that Gilo had a gun on him.

'You ride with us, amigo. We talk with men in your house.'

Trav threw himself sideways into the rocks, drawing his gun as he fell. The roar of Gilo's shot shattered the darkness. Flint splinters splashed. He fired once at Gilo, saw the shadow go down. The Indian faded. Trav sent a bullet where he had last seen the dark movement. Gilo's next gun slug burned past

206

Trav's face. Trav leveled another shot at Gilo. This time the shadow did not get up. A rifle bullet sang from the cut. Trav sent a shot toward the sound of the report. He heard hoof stumblings on stones, a running horse. Hawktree vanished into the night, the hoofbeats dying northward.

Inside the cave, Trav relighted the lamp. He stood near the opening and threw the glass bowl against the stack of wooden crates. The fuel splashed out, with flames following in a dozen places. Fire crawled rapidly over the rifle boxes. He walked downgrade, past Gilo's still form, up the slope, and limped to the house.

Mary and Wilda watched over his shoulder when he faced the night. They all saw it, the dark column of smoke lifting in the arroyo, laced with sparks from the cave. Comanche eyes would see it, too. They heard the first dull explosions of the ammunition. As he barred the door again from inside, he had the small satisfaction that one rifle consignment, at least, would never reach the Comanches.

'We've spread the rifles around,' Mary told. him. 'There's at least one at every window.'

Wilda's voice turned softer than he had ever heard it. 'Just in case they make it a little bad for us at daylight, Trav, I want you to know— the kid's told me. She's in love with you.'

'Wilda!'

Trav probed for the slight shoulders in the

207

darkness. He got an arm about them and drew Mary close to him.

They worked calmly in the night, following Trav's directions, preparing for what he knew would happen at dawn. Trav realized that a quick Comanche count of three rifles firing from the cabin would be fatal to the three of them in fast order.

He secured eleven rifle barrels to eleven portholes in the trick shutters by driving in improvised wedges cut from the wood packing cases, keeping one weapon free for his own use. He lashed the stock ends to rests on chair backs, a bedstead, or to rope lengths suspended from the rafters. The rifles were leveled for an aim he calculated to be horsebelly high, but aim was only secondary.

'We've got to make it sound like an army in here,' he explained. 'Twelve rifles going off at one time. That means twelve men.' And it would mean a vital difference in Comanche calculations. Three rifles—maybe two of them doubtful in both speed of fire and targets—would mean one thing to the smart warriors. It would confirm Hawktree's report that the Smith forces were absent, that a stranger had burned the rifles and that the house was weakly manned. But a burst of twelve rifles would be impressive. 'You don't have to hit anything,' Trav said. 'Maybe you will, maybe not. Luck ought to get us a pony or two. All we want is to fool 'em. Otherwise, they'll hit that door about the second charge they make and walk right in for breakfast. Now let's rehearse.'

He took a make-believe sight into the night, then waved his arm behind him. He turned, watching the dim figures of the girls. Wilda pantomimed a pull on a cluster of rope strands gathered in her hand, and Trav did the same with another string. The strands led to rifle triggers. 'Theoretically, twelve rifles fired then,' he said. 'What do you do, Mary?'

She hurried from one window to the next, making the motions of working rifle levers. 'I would do this. You and Wilda would be tightening your trigger strings for the next pull.'

'We can do it fifteen times without reloading magazines.' Trav commented. 'That's a lot of shootin'—then we've got to reload. Fast!'

It was all he could think to do. Not much, maybe. Better than the alternative of three guns pecking at swirling streaks of yelling savages, giving themselves away by their puny numbers. It kept them busy through the nervous hours. That counted for something.

He took a quick look through his porthole at the approaching dawn.

Two women. Just himself and two girls. Sisters who had nothing in common until a circumstance like this had brought them closer together than ever before in their lives. Well, he had hated, too. Hated the man who had robbed him, hated the white men who had blackened his name and turned suspicion upon him. Yet, in this moment, much of that seemed drained out, no longer vital as it used to be.

His world hung on a slender thread of whether he could scheme, fight, trigger, and reload well enough to keep the painted, kill-minded savages out of this house. This was all that counted. Life had not been too good, in the past, for any of them. Now he knew a craving for more of it, a white man's instinct to hang on, to cling to the condition called being alive. He'd known it before in Indian fights, in the Tonkawa camp when he thought he was dying. Now it was the same, but with something added. Now there was Mary.

CHAPTER FIFTEEN

First the three saddle ponies in the corral were driven out. Then smoke boiled up in the gray-black night. The long bunkhouse caved in amidst searing flames and the corral shed at the same time. An apparition with paint-daubed body who jogged out bearing a saddle in his arms was the first Comanche to go down in the gloomy dawn. Trav fired just once—a single vindictive shot, because of the saddle the Comanche carried. After that, the rock house was silent. The Comanches faded in the haze.

'Keep holding your fire. That rush was just their feeler, their cat's paw.' Trav closed the porthole. 'Maybe the next one. Maybe we'll pull a few rifle strings then.'

The stark fear on the two faces touched him to the quick. He had to prepare them better. He had to go on talking until the big attack came.

'You've got to keep from looking,' Trav said, long enough to absorb the first shock. It's the sight of them, the way they come at you, that does the damage.'

Later, they could look. Time would come when they would have to bend to the portholes and fire the Henry repeaters on targets, the slow way, but the best they could.

'You may think you see horses running around without riders,' he said. 'Now, don't—'

'How do they ride that way, shooting all the time?' Mary asked.

'The Comanches will be hanging over the other side, out of target. That's the way they do. But that marksmanship legend is bunk. These are savages, remember. Warlike children, with a kid's weakness for showing off. This is a performance, the way their brain works it. They think they're accomplishing something by hugging the off-side of their ponies and trying to shoot under the necks. In a way, an Indian is a damn fool. Nearly every

211

time he gets funny, that way, he loses a little more of the land he used to have. But they keep on showing off.'

'But I've always heard that they circle and kill everybody without making a target of themselves.'

'Settlers get excited. That's natural. What happens in a fight is a panicky blur. Survivors are apt to exaggerate later. That business about Indians hanging half-off a running horse and shooting a rifle or bow and arrow under the horse's head is mostly fictitious. They go through the motions but they don't hit anything. Ask any old buffalo hunter or Indian fighter. That story's been going the rounds on the plains ever since the first whites got into trouble. It's just a tall tale. No Comanche born is a natural rifleman. In the Rangers, we practiced on firing ranges for days at a time. So does the Federal cavalry. No Indians ever had that much ammunition or ambition. Everything about a rifle is foreign to them.'

'I'd always heard the Comanches were great marksmen,' Wilda said.

'Working a rifle is just not in their line. Aiming and the slow trigger squeeze are all that count, and these savages can't do it. Just the job of cleaning a rifle, keeping it in good shape, is bad enough chore for a white man. Indians don't know how, don't care. What whips the whites is the yells and the noise and the big numbers.'

*   *   *

He had given them what advice and support he could. Now dawn had come, and the feeler attack, and they would need all the confidence they could hang on to when the real wave of hell came flooding the doorstep.

His eyes held to the barrel of the rifle, and from the muzzle bead to the mass of brown bodies on running horses boiling up in the dawn. The Comanches strung their ponies out in a circle, engulfing the yard. Painted bodies disappeared to the off-side of the ponies. The earth shook to the rattle of hoofs, rifle fire and screeching yells. Bullets splattered the stone walls.

He waited. The sight started a cold sweat. He fought down a panicky urge to start throwing lead at random. The thing to do was to watch for their break for the house. And here they came now, the first sudden turn of the wheeling riders, a whooping mass bearing down upon door and windows. It would be the same on the other side. Trav pulled a bead on the front rider, saw him topple to the ground under meat-chopper hoofs. Trav waved his arm behind him as a signal.

Grabbing the twine lengths gathered loosely over a wall peg at his side, he pulled on the strands all together and five rifles from that wall boomed a staccato.

213

A war pony floundered and went down.

At the same instant, Wilda stood back and pulled her cluster of similar trigger lines. Six rifles went off on that side. Turning to check, Trav noted that the kick had loosened one rifle from its moorings, leaving its muzzle pointed to the outside sky. But that wouldn't matter too much. He saw Mary speed down the line, working the Henry levers like lightning, while Wilda took the slack out of the trigger strings again. Mary darted across the room to work the other five on that side, and Trav squinted through for a glimpse of the melee just outside.

The tide of jumbled riders went tearing out to the yard again, some of them firing back at the windows. A slug bit deep into the shutter above Travs head, with splinters flying. He took pinpoint aim on a tail-end rider and triggered off the shot just below the feathered headpiece. The warrior pitched head down and was carried off with feet hung, head bumping the ground at each leap of the panicked pony. Trav signaled, and pulled the gun strings as if he were see-sawing a double mule span. Eleven more shots boomed from the rock walls.

As he made the rounds of the windows, studying the vacant distances now showing streaks of sun light, he wondered how long it could go on. No way to anticipate the Comanche mind. They did crazy things. They might think of—other business and pull out quickly. They might try at the house all morning, finally pecking resistance to pieces. If they ever stormed a window or two, or got to the door in any numbers, a break-through would be certain. It was easier to pray that they would pull out before the sun drifted high.

They looked at each other in the gloom, squinting through layers of powder smoke. In this lull, a far-off shot sounded, a random bullet flattened itself against stone. This was on the girls' side, and Wilda bent to peer through a porthole. The young bucks who foolishly fired from out of sight, sending vagrant shots houseward during the lull, could not have aimed at any particular spot. The next bullet was nothing but a stray, and the force of it must have been almost spent when it chanced to find its way into the exact crack where the wood edges of the window shutters met. The mushy sound lost itself among other sporadic bullet smashes against stone. Mary was handing a cup of water to Trav, and he was tightening the moorings at the propped-up stock of one of the repeaters, when Wilda spoke quietly from across the room.

'I think I'm shot.'

She was sitting on the edge of a chair, stiffly erect, eyes puzzled, a tight fist pressed to her chest. Before Trav took two paces, Wilda relaxed, leaned back, dropped her hand. Her glance up at him was apologetic. 'Something hit here,' she said, and her eyelids fluttered.

They saw the dark stain beginning to spread in her shirt front. Dropping to her knees, Mary caught at her sister's clothes, tore into the shirt to find the wound. Wilda's hand stopped her.

'It hurts,' Wilda breathed. Her lips worked thickly. Her next words were barely audible. 'Everything is so far away.'

Her eyes flicked open, found Trav's face above. 'I'm sorry—Trav—about everything.'

'It's all right, Wilda.'

'You and Mary—'

There were no more words, nor breath to say them with. Wilda let go all her tension, and her head hung limply down. The stiffness went out of her arms, and she appeared to have gone peacefully to sleep.

Trav carried her body to the bed and covered it with a blanket. He returned to find Mary hurriedly gathering the loose trigger lines while tears trickled down her cheeks.

'I think they're coming again,' she sobbed. 'Look over here.'

But this was no formation of the Comanche force for a new attack. He saw them bunching in the edge of the first scrub trees a mile out. But their attention seemed to be away from the house, toward a lift of approaching dust. Soon he made out the band of horsemen. A feathered chief rode to meet them. Then he knew the rider on the big red horse who headed the newcomers.

He whirled to see Mary wiping back a tear,

216

her face turned toward the blanketed form visible in the other room. 'Poor Wilda! I guess she had a little good in her. It seems so—such a shocking thing to have to happen.'

'You be real strong, now,' he said firmly. 'I've got to tell you something.'

'I'm strong.' She knuckled each smoke-stained eye and made her quivering chin raise to him.

'The Comanches have got reinforcements,' he said huskily. 'Denver Smith and his little army have just arrived.'

Mary's gasp of dismay matched the sick feeling in his own middle. With the Comanches only to deal with, they might have worn the redskin patience thin, until the warriors thought of something better to do somewhere else. Now the assault would be relentless. There would be white men's brains, Denver Smith's knowledge of the house, and of the defenders, to guide Comanche brutality. He and Mary alone could not keep them out for long. They would be reduced to firing one rifle at a time, trying to make their shots count. Maybe they could stand off the next assault, maybe the one after that. The end would be the same.

And that's the way the strange battle unreeled itself. Denver Smith and Dog combined red and white tactics. The combined force that thundered down was too big to fight off. Trav and Mary pumped their shots at the

217

mass, but a door edge splintered from the smashes of a battering ram. The high yells outside, the gunsmoke, milling ponies, riflemen, now included Smith's white crew. The yard turned into a maelstrom of horror. A window on the other side began to smoke from fire on the outside. Somewhere down the room near Wilda's deathbed a shutter strained under repeated heavy smashings. Trav sent a bullet at the crack of it, aiming through powder-smoke clouds. Mary threw a bucket of water against the smoking shutter. Trav spotted Denver's slyly placed porthole at the bottom of the door, and poked a rifle barrel through it, levering twice, sending two bullets somewhere into a jumble of legs. Howls arose and the door ramming stopped. But he had to hurry back to a porthole, and then the assault on the door started anew. He emptied one rifle after another.

Now the entire Comanche force and their white allies were bunched against the walls, and it was difficult to draw an aim at those angles. Red-painted bodies lay here and there in the weeds, and a white one. But not enough to make any difference in the outcome.

'Just the door,' Trav finally called to Mary. Her powder-streaked chin acknowledged this. They backed away, facing the big wooden slab, and squeezed off their shots where the first splintered crack had broken through. The battering stopped again. Above the din there,

Trav heard the judge's shout: 'Hit the other door—the other side! Hit 'em both at once, damn you!' There came a flurry of sound passing around the house, and then a battering started on the opposite door.

Mary pointed. Another window shutter was smoking now. Trav sent a bullet through its crack, another into the split at the door in front of him. Mary was levering her rifle at the west porthole. His own hammer fell upon an empty chamber.

All at once a dead silence. They were'standing almost back to back, when he turned. 'This rifle is empty!' she gasped. 'All those are empty on this side.'

He caught up one, motioned for ammunition, feverishly beginning the reloading. Twelve empty rifles. The delay would be costly.

The battering went on at both doors, with splintered cracks appearing. Smoke from a shutter mingled with rifle smoke to make the room stifling. After he loaded two magazines, he handed a rifle to Mary, and they retreated to a corner, crouching side by side with rifles ready for the first door break-through. The rest was just a matter of time. There were too many of them, too many weak spots to watch, not enough time for another reloading.

Denver Smith's voice bellowed out again, shouting an order. A gobble of Comanche yells. A new rain of bullets. Lead splashed through cracks and portholes and knocked stone slivers from the inside walls.

Mary's hand went down into her bosom, out again, clutching the little derringer Rotan had returned to her. Trav nodded grimly. 'But not till after the door gives. Not till I tell you.'

They held their fire, with fifteen shots left apiece for the first inpouring when a door went down. They'd never live to get off that many, he knew. The first ones through the break would have to die, but the crazed tide behind them would fill the room and that would be the end.

A painted face showed at the loosened, burning shutter toward the corner. Trav splashed the face back with a quick shot. Mary pressed tight against him, rifle ready, her white, drawn features fixed paralyzed on the door. The battering ram hit a mighty smash, then, and more splintered cracks showed sunlight.

They raised their rifles in readiness.

'Break it in, now!' Denver Smith's voice bellowed.

White and red voices responded in a yelling prelude to triumph. And as Trav and Mary waited for the next smash to tear the door from its hinges, the outside commotion changed key, rose again, died off. For a mystifying moment, quietness came.

The yells shrilled out again, but in a different note. The battering at the door stopped. Straining to hear, Trav caught the confusion of sounds, running feet, short yelps of surprise, a flurry of movement, horses, frantic voices.

Springing to a window, Trav put his eye cautiously to a porthole. Then his muscles went stiff and his breath choked up in his chest. Mumbling, he summoned Mary to the window beside him.

'Look! Quick—out there!'

Besides the mystifying fire power the three defenders had been able to throw at the Comanches on their initial assaults, the later settlers on the Staked Plain also remembered the 'Battle of Brazos Pass' for the strangest alignment of opposing forces in all the Indian battles of the West. Before it ended, white and red men were fighting together against enemies of their same colors. Tonkawas against Comanches. Fort Belknap Rangers against Denver Smith's *comancheros*.

And Trav and Mary saw them coming, only seconds after the Smith army and Dog's redskins sighted them—the Rangers and the Tonks, in two formations, and Lige Drain and the Cap Rock nesters, pouring out of the brush and cuts to the southeast, a long charging line of gun-bristling horsemen. The Tonkawa yells screeched through the moming, drowning all other sounds.

The resultant confusion among the surprised besiegers at the house was partially to blame for their near massacre. The other factor was that Captain Small dispersed his Rangers, letting the Tonkawas under Blue Knife hit first, while the Rangers spread out, cutting off break-through escape of both the Comanches and Smith's forces.

With a choking sensation, even though he kept pumping bullets at stray targets of panicked Comanches running for safety, Trav recognized Captain Small, and then he saw Rotan with a smoking Winchester in the thick of it, and old Blue Knife when the ancient chief went down under churning hoofs from a Comanche bullet. And then, after a time, the yard was near silent, the only sounds coming from far off where the last desultory shooting followed the handful of Comanche survivors.

With Mary beside him, Trav pushed to the splintered door, lifted the bar, and cautiously swung it open, his Colt in hand. Mary gasped. He followed her downward glance and saw the whipcord-clad body, the big, prone length of the mustached white man.

Denver Smith lay dead. The pulpy bullet hole showed through his shirt as the Brazos czar stretched in the dust of his own yard, gazing sunward with unblinking eyes. The little stain seeped out until blood touched his jacket lapel and the wilted dab of bluebonnets there.

Trav looked at the sixgun in his own hand, the heavy, black .45 that had been Old Man Bradshaw's, and slowly holstered it. Maybe, considering everything, it had avenged the bad times of the past, with the Lord taking care of another self-appointed land ruler in His own way.

In the northern breaks he sighted the Ranger force loping back. Looking past the burnt corral shed, the smoldering bunkhouse ruins, over the scattering of brown and white dead in the yard weeds, he saw the familiarly thin shape of Captain Small, with burly Rotan riding beside him. Together, he and Mary watched, too taut in their emotions to speak. Captain Small and Rotan pulled ahead, galloped their horses down the slope and up again. When they were close enough, both raised their rifles to wave a greeting.

'Howdy, Ranger!' Small bellowed in his hoarse voice. Rotan grinned broadly. He had done his job well, his expression said, and he wanted Trav to know it. A big chunk of Texas had been opened that morning for the settlers who would push west now across the Brazos, with the barrier at Brazos Pass removed.

But it was after their handshakes all around, and the commending words of Captain Small had been gruffly spoken, that Trav and Mary walked hand-in-hand to the distant cedars. They only glanced at the bodies they passed, until they found the small crumpled corpse in its bloody deerskin trappings and feathered headdress.

After a time, they turned away from the

chieftain from the Territory who had made his last ride at the head of his diminishing tribe of Tonkawas.

'It's what he came to do,' Trav murmured. 'He died the way he wanted it. Fighting the Comanches.'

They walked aimlessly away from the unpleasant sight of twisted shapes dotting the approaches to the ranch yard. The sun beamed from high-up blue, and the powder smell dissolved a little under the cleansing of an April breeze off the Cap Rock.

'Blue Knife saved my life once,' Trav said. 'Then he came back and helped save it again. He threw in with the Rangers when Rotan guided them out. I guess Smith's army was mighty confused when they saw Tonks and Rangers and nesters coming at them all at once.'

Mary's strained face searched up to him. The freckled, pinched cheeks showed a tinge of pink, but laughter stirred deep in the blue eyes.

'Blue Knife told me,' she said shyly. 'When you were getting horses in their camp for our ride here. About Beelah. The twenty ponies. You turned his gift back to the tribe.'

He had to smile at that. 'Blue Knife thought you were my woman, Mary.'

Her hands caught at his shoulders. Her face buried itself to his chest.

'I am,' Mary whispered.

We hope you have enjoyed this Large Print book. Other Chivers Press or G.K. Hall & Co. Large Print books are available at your library or directly from the publishers.

For more information about current and forthcoming titles, please call or write, without obligation, to:

Chivers Press Limited
Windsor Bridge Road
Bath BA2 3AX
England
Tel. (01225) 335336

OR

G.K. Hall & Co.
P.O. Box 159
Thorndike, Maine 04986
USA
Tel. (800) 223-2336

All our Large Print titles are designed for easy reading, and all our books are made to last.